Invite to a Showdown

Terrell L. Bowers

A Black Horse Western

ROBERT HALE · LONDON

ISBN 978-0-7090-9638-2

Robert Hale Limited
Clerkenwell House
Clerkenwell Green
London EC1R 0HT

www.halebooks.com

Typeset by
Derek Doyle & Associates, Shaw Heath
Printed and bound in Great Britain by
CPI Antony Rowe, Chippenham and Eastbourne

CHAPTER ONE

In August of 1862 the escalation of the Civil War, and a mix-up over when money was due, caused a delay in payment to the Sioux living at the Yellow Medicine and Redwood Falls Agencies in western Minnesota. The Sioux were near starving because of poor crops and had been counting on their guaranteed annual compensation for survival.

A rather insignificant incident – a farmer admonished some Indian boys for stealing eggs – sparked a bloody reprisal. The Sioux, under the powerful chief, Little Crow, declared war against all whites. His bands, along with several others, went on the warpath, killing and terrorizing settlers from western Minnesota, throughout parts of Iowa and over into eastern Dakota. Over the next three months, they slaughtered an estimated 750 white settlers, while taking over 200 girls and women into captivity. The hostages were horribly treated, but spared death, so that they could be sold for ransom or used as bargaining power against a pursuing army.

Rowena Janson had been the only survivor from their farm. She might have been killed during the raid, but she was slight of build and her baby face belied her actual twelve years of age. Seeing her two older brothers and parents murdered before her eyes, she collapsed in a state of shock. One of the braves found her curled into a fetal ball, but when he shook her awake Rowena simply stared blindly and said nothing. Thinking she must be retarded or even crazy, he took her as a captive.

Fortunately for Rowena she didn't become fully conscious of her surroundings until after she was thrust inside a holding area, where there were many other women and children. Suffering under the excruciating weight of grief and terror, now left completely alone in the world, she broke down and sobbed.

A motherly woman took pity on her. She held her close and comforted her until she recovered her senses. She also shielded her from view of any passing Indians.

'Hush now,' the woman advised her once Rowena was composed. 'I saw the way they brung you here. One of the Indians gestured to some others that

6

you were not right in the head.'

Rowena sniffed back the last of her tears. 'I-I don't remember anything, not after I seen my mother. . . .' She couldn't get out the words.

'You want to get through this, you have to be strong,' the woman told her. 'You do exactly as I say and I think you'll be left alone.'

Rowena used what strength she could muster and looked up at the woman. 'What do you mean?'

'My husband once told me that most Indians will not harm a crazy person. So long as they think you're not right in the head, they'll leave you be. Do you hear what I'm telling you?'

Rowena frowned. 'Yes, but what does that have to do with me?'

The lady exhibited a sympathetic smile. Her hair was twisted and mussed, she had a bruise on her cheek and a deep scratch showed where her dress had been torn off one shoulder. Regarding Rowena with sincere blue eyes, she explained.

'Listen to me, child,' she murmured softly. 'You must pretend you are dull-witted. It's the best chance you have.'

'You mean, make everyone think I'm crazy?' Rowena asked.

Looking around quickly, making sure none of the captors were watching, the lady leaned over and whispered instructions into her ear. Rowena listened and nodded her head. Then the woman stood up. 'I can't speak to you again, or they might suspect you are pretending. Be strong, dear girl,' was her advice. 'This will be over one day soon. The soldiers will come for us.'

Rowena didn't have time to say thanks. Several Indians suddenly burst into their midst and the lady and several of the others were taken away. A few other braves, some quite young, came in among them, taunting, manhandling and examining the remainder of the hostages. Most of the remaining girls were quite young or mere children. Two or three of the older ones were selected and dragged out of the enclosure, but not Rowena. She did as the woman had suggested and no one touched her. As for those unfortunate women who were chosen, a few never returned . . . including the sweet lady who had warned her.

Rowena faithfully stuck to her deception whenever her captors were around. Shutting out everything around her, she would sit down, wrap her arms across her chest, and begin to rock back and forth. It took all of her courage, but she willed herself to sing the lullaby her mother had taught her.

One time an Indian youth, who was likely in his mid-teens, came by and poked her with a stick. Although the jab hurt, she hesitated only long enough to start her song over. Summoning all of her willpower Rowena pretended he wasn't there.

Unconvinced, the brave knelt down and sneered at her, saying something harsh, which she did not understand. Rowena ignored him, keeping her eyes focused in the distance, while she continued to rock and sing. He gave a yank of her hair, causing her to gasp in pain. However, as soon as he let go, she returned to the ruse once more, rocking and singing.

He snarled his contempt, tossed a handful of dirt at her, then spun away and went looking for someone else to torment.

For several weeks that was Rowena's existence. Whenever one or more of the Indians were near by or watching she sat and rocked herself while she hummed or sang. The only time she stopped was to eat. With only meager rations of food, she dared not pretend at feeding time, as other prisoners would gladly have eaten her share. Late at nights was her only respite, when she could be certain none of her abductors was around. Then she would huddle in the single blanket provided, shiver from the cold, and grieve for the loss of her family.

The woman who had warned her was the last person who tried to speak to her. Most of the hostages crowded together for solace. Rowena wondered what happened to some of the hostages. She heard murmurs that several had died from mistreatment by the captors, while others perished from malnutrition or illness. Many times the cries of those chosen by the warriors could be heard from the tepees. Most of the women returned weeping or somber, but several were not seen again. It was a nightmare without end.

Rowena marched along with the others whenever the camp was moved and ate the food provided. When their captors ran out of goods they had stolen during their raids they provided only seed-cakes, dried roots and berries, along with tiny bits of nearly raw meat. For drinking it was often necessary to eat handfuls of snow. Rowena grew weak physically from the bad food and frigid conditions, but remained strong in spirit.

The diet caused many to fall sick; to become too ill to walk meant being taken away and never seen again. The weather was wet, cold and miserable, but Rowena endured the hardships and survived.

The harsh winter, trying to provide for so many prisoners over several months, and the dogged pursuit of the soldiers finally wore down Little Crow. As time passed, and lacking aid from many of the tribes, his warriors began to desert. Once all of the captive women and children arrived at Little Crow's camp he was faced with a no-win situation. It was time to make peace.

Colonel Sibley had been sent to squash the rebellion, leading a combined force of about 1,600 men, including infantry, cavalry and some artillery. After a few minor skirmishes and fights with the Indians, Sibley sent word to Little Crow to surrender.

Little Crow, having started the war without the approval of any other chiefs, lacked support from several important tribes. Now cornered, his warriors began slipping away to return to their homes. Little Crow was forced to agreed to Sibley's terms for surrender even though it meant turning over most of his remaining warriors to the army.

The hostages were eventually freed at the appropriately named Camp Release. It had been several long months for the hostages. Most of the women were left without husbands and all had lost family members and friends. Upon their release the prisoners returned to relatives or people who would help them salvage their lives. Some of the children, like Rowena, were left without any family or friends at all.

Desperate to have the situation resolved, the authorities in charge were eager to turn a child over to anyone who would care for it. It was easier than trying to figure out what to do with a sizeable number of orphans.

Rowena was one of the last in camp, unaware of any living relatives or close friends. She gravely awaited the decision as to whether she would be sent to an orphan home or be placed with one of the ex-captive women, some of whom were accepting the responsibility of an extra child or two. Of course, those who had seen her during captivity actually believed she was sick in her mind. None of them volunteered to take the 'crazy girl' with them.

At last a hunter and scout recently mustered out of the army, named Jethro 'Buckeye' Summerville, approached the man in charge and said he would take Rowena. He explained that he had a sickly wife, who needed help around the house, and they would look after the homeless child. The army remanded her into his custody at once, glad to have one less waif to worry about.

Buckeye only had one horse and his own personal gear. He had Rowena ride behind him until they reached a trading post. There he was able to buy a pack-mule and he bartered for her a large buffalo coat. Although it was much too big for her, Rowena would be able to wrap it about her legs to keep her feet warm and dry.

Once the supplies were packed Buckeye lifted Rowena up and placed her on the mule. He hadn't said much to her since the hasty adoption, but now he offered her a smile.

'We've got a long way to go, little squirrel,' he said. 'I hope you can handle the long hours of travel.'

'I won't be any trouble,' she replied.

It was the very first words she had said to him. Buckeye squinted up at her. With his full beard it was difficult to discern his expression, but it appeared that a crooked smile lifted the corners of his mouth.

'You ain't one bit crazy, are you.' He made it a statement.

'A lady warned me to act like I wasn't right in the head so the Indians would let me alone.'

'Clever lady,' he praised. 'Yep, she done you a good turn with that advice.'

'Where are we going?'

Buckeye took a tobacco plug out of his shirt pocket and bit off a wad. He began to chew, but stopped long enough to answer. 'I've got a cabin way to hell ... uh,' he hastily corrected his language, 'that is, way off yonder. We'll hold up there till spring and then mosey up to the northern plains. In the summer months we can make us enough from buffalo hunting to live year around.' He worked the chaw to one side and rotated his head. He spat a stream of juice on to the trail.

'See that?' he asked her. Rowena frowned, wondering what he meant, but he clarified: 'Takes practice for a bearded gent to spit tobacca without getting any in his whiskers.'

She took note that there were no stains among the grizzled black hair of his beard. 'You must practice a lot.'

He laughed. 'I'll dig you out a couple strips of jerky. You can chew on them when you get hungry. Way I travel, we grab a bite each morning and don't stop till dark. That means you don't want to be drinking too much water.' He cocked one bushy eyebrow. 'You know why, don't you?'

She thought for a moment and then bobbed her head. 'So we don't stop for walks into the brush.'

'Flying buffalo chips!' he exclaimed. 'You're smart as a whip.' He passed her several pieces of jerky and said, 'You and me are going to get along just fine.'

'What about your sick wife?'

'I reckon I might have given that soldier boy the wrong impression. I was really talking about you taking care of me, not a wife – which I haven't got.'

'I'm beholden to you for giving me a home,' Rowena managed, speaking with as much maturity as she could manage.

'I know I ain't no replacement for your family, little squirrel, but I'll sure enough see you don't starve or freeze, and I'll treat you good.' Buckeye made the promise and then turned for his horse. It

14

was time to get started.

The wind was cold and a storm appeared headed on their way, but Rowena put her trust in the ex-scout. Buckeye seemed an honorable man, and she was determined to make the best of her situation. His cabin was several hundred miles away, and it would be a long trip, but she would endure the hardships without complaint. Once they reached Buckeye's cabin she would learn to cook, gather and chop wood, and keep his house in order. There was a lot to learn and a lot of winter left, but Rowena had a new home.

CHAPTER TWO

January 1864

For three years Travis Clay did his duty, fighting for the Yankee forces across a dozen states. Ready and willing to take command of 'most any situation, Travis rose in rank to a sergeant. He was promoted to a second lieutenant when he saved the lives of a colonel and several other men during a botched attack. As more officers fell in battle, he moved up to captain and soon had his own company of men. Along the way he became fast friends with a mature fellow everyone called 'Sparky'. His actual name was Spartan Vogel, son of a Greek mother and half-Dutch father. He could talk the ears off a corn stalk, but he was a man who took orders and saw that other men obeyed as well. Clay insisted Sparky remain under his command every time he was promoted to a higher rank.

Throughout the endless months of fighting and marching, 'most every man suffered from poor rations, bouts of dysentery, and numerous other miseries that sapped a man's strength during the bitter cold of winter or the sweltering heat of summer. It was part of war, part of the unending privation that made war something to be avoided except as a last resort.

There were many skirmishes against the Confederates, but more men died from bad water, tainted food and infection than were killed outright from bullets or shrapnel. Travis and Sparky stuck it out together, determined to see the end of slavery and a reuniting of the States.

For the final push of the war Travis and Sparky were assigned to Brigadier General Alfred Terry. The men under his command were a mix from numerous backgrounds, but they had grown together as a unit, having spent several campaigns living, fighting and surviving together. This engagement was rumored to be part of the final push. If the Union Army could take Fort Fisher, General Lee would be cut off from the rest of his army, pushed back to Petersburg with only a few thousand Confederate soldiers. It could mean the end of the war.

Terry sent a division of United States Colored Troops to hold off any advance or support from

Confederate forces from north of Fort Fisher. Then he coordinated a full-scale attack on the Rebel stronghold with the Navy.

Fort Fisher was heavily fortified, over a mile in length, situated between Cape Fear River and the Atlantic Ocean. It had sand walls along the waterfront twenty-five feet thick, which could repel even the heavy cannon shot from a Navy bombardment. And these were a determined lot of Confederates.

The Navy sent 2,000 sailors and Marines to storm the northeast salient, but the fort defenses rallied to completely shut down the assault from that direction. Using the Navy's siege as a diversionary tactic, Terry launched his division of 4,000 troops in an attack against the northern end of the fort.

Being in one of the companies near the front of the assault, Travis and Sparky were immediately engaged in deadly combat with the Rebel forces. The Confederates rallied fiercely and turned cannon and gunfire against the new wave of Unionist troops.

The blasts from cannon shook the earth, the impact of each shell spewing fire and smoke, while shrapnel tore through flesh and bone of the charging soldiers. A great volley of gunfire preceded the screams and wails of those who were hit. It was like leading an assault through the gates of hell.

Travis urged his company forward against the

heavy gunfire and shelling as hundreds of gallant men were felled during the charge. The bloody fighting continued; there could be no retreat. This was the final thrust, the quickest way to end the war that had torn the country apart. They had to gain control of the fort in order to force General Lee and the remnants of his army into a corner.

Smoke and dust filled the air and the dying wail of men could be heard over the explosions. The battle raged long and hard – the men forced to fight hand-to-hand – before the Confederate troops were finally overwhelmed.

It was full dark, only an hour or two before midnight when the Rebels eventually surrendered. Travis looked around and discovered that his lieutenant had been killed. He told Sparky to make an inventory of his remaining men, though he dreaded hearing the number of casualties. Sparky was gone twenty minutes and returned with a detailed head count. He offered up the report shortly after midnight.

'Of our one hundred and forty-six men, we have sixty-three ready for duty, and another fifteen to twenty carrying some minor wounds. Seventeen are severely injured and probably won't make another roll call. The remainder didn't make it.'

'So many good men, Sparky,' Travis lamented. 'We paid an ungodly price to take this fort.'

'Word has it the sailors and Marines took a worse beating. They never got closer than a few hundred feet. The bodies on that side are stacked like cord-wood for a hard winter.'

'I saw Jensen and Caulter go down.'

'Yeah,' Sparky replied sadly. 'I remember you saying both of those boys came from down near your neck of the woods. It looks like you'll be riding home alone.'

'What a tragic and devastating war,' Travis lamented. 'I signed up with seven other men to fight for freedom together. Now I'm the only one left.'

'At least, you know two of them were only wounded, although the younger boy probably lost his leg. I 'spect they are both back home, wondering if this war will ever end.'

'Bivouac the men and made sure our injured are being looked after. I've got to make a report to HQ.'

'Better watch it, Capt'n,' Sparky warned. 'They might try and pin another bar on your shoulders.'

Travis grinned. 'No chance of that. This is supposed to be our last major battle. The only bars I'm looking for are the *bar counters* at the saloons we might stop by at on our way home.'

'Aye, Capt'n. You go do your officer type stuff whilst I pick out a soft spot for us to bunk. I'll have a bed ready by the time you get back.'

Travis gave him a nod and headed to the officers' tent. The smell of blood and acrid smoke hung over the compound. Even the sea breeze carried the scent of suffering and death. The end of slavery had come at a terrible price.

Rowena paused to arch her back, stiff from bending over. She wiped her brow and spoke to Buckeye. 'I'm getting real tired of smelling like blood and guts all of the time.'

He paused from his own chore and grinned. 'The money is good; it's about the only way we can earn a living.' Buckeye had downed six buffalo before the herd moved out of range. Rowena had skinned four. He put a note of encouragement in his voice.

'Only two more to go, Squirrel. Then we can take the hides and sellable meat back to town. Once we fetch the money for our goods, we're done for the winter.'

A tight little frown crossed her face. 'That seller tried to cheat you last time. I don't trust him no further than you can spit.'

Buckeye laughed. 'Yep, his face turned red as a ripe apple when you pointed out how he had not carried the one when running the total. It would have cost us ten dollars, if not for you being a wizard at adding numbers.'

'You are moving real stiff again today,' Rowena

observed. 'Reminds me of someone trying to walk barefoot over a pile of eggs.'

'It's just a touch of ruematiz. Nothing to worry about.'

'That there rheumatism has gotten worse each year and specially seems troublesome come a spell of cold or wet weather. Good thing this is our last hunt of the season, or else your legs might stop working altogether.'

'I'm glad it's our last hunt too, Squirrel. We've earned enough this season to put another few dollars away for my retirement and still be flush for the winter.'

Turning the blade of her knife to the angle needed, she once more bent over the buffalo. 'Only two more critters to go.' She sighed. 'Then I ain't even gonna think about one of these mangy critters till next spring.'

'Back to our little hideaway to spend the winter,' Buckeye agreed. 'I'm looking forward to putting my feet up and taking it easy.'

In her mind Rowena pictured the little mountain cabin where they spent the worst of the winter months. It was the first home she had known after Buckeye took her from Camp Release. Built of logs, with a thatch roof and a small cooking-stove and two rooms, it was warm and dry during the harsh weather. It was located a few miles from a trading post, over at a place known as Beaver Creek. There was abundant game in the area, lots of trees, with different bushes that produced berries, and along the creek she could usually find wild onions, straw-berries and edible roots. In another year or two Buckeye would retire from hunting. Then the little place would be their home year around.

No more camping on the trail for months on end, no sleeping out in the open or trying to stay dry under a lean-to. How wonderful to get up and start a fire to warm the house, then to cook on the little stove, with no wind blowing dust into the vittles. To be able to have a clean bed, to sit down proper to eat, to be protected from the weather – yes, it was something she looked forward to.

When news arrived of Lee's surrender it was like a dozen Christmas mornings all combined into one. The celebration of the unit lasted for two days solid, and spirits were even higher when orders arrived a few months later to muster the volunteers out of the army.

'What are you figuring to do, Capt'n?' Sparky asked Travis, after learning of the news. 'You going to give up this life of luxury and being an important man?'

Travis smiled. The two of them were in his officer's tent, sharing it because no one had been appointed to replace his lieutenant. 'I've had enough fighting and killing to last a lifetime,' he replied. 'I imagine I'll try and get a job somewhere, maybe working on the railroad or hauling freight or something.'

'You remember I told you about my sister and how she lives over in Colorado?' At a nod from Travis, Sparky continued: 'Her last letter said they were having a little trouble; a couple of their hired help has quit or been run off.'

'I thought they had themselves a fair-sized ranch?'

'Some joker named Armstrong moved in and wants more than his fair share of the valley. I don't know all of what's been going on, but my sis says Armstrong has been doing a lot of pushing. She needs a couple men who know how to push back.'

'Long way to go for a fight,' Travis said. 'Didn't we both agree not to get involved in any more wars?'

'It ain't like I'm trying to hire you because you're a good man in a fight,' Sparky said. 'I mean, they're short-handed and need a couple good men. When I left to join the Union Army they had six riders working there. Now it's a couple old pals of mine trying to do everything by themselves.'

'Sparky, the only thing I know about cattle is which steak I most enjoy. Besides which, I've never

24

been west of Nebraska.'

'You said yourself that you had no kin left, no place to call your home.' Sparky snorted. 'Well, here's your chance to get a fresh start. Working alongside three old men, you'll be the ramrod in no time.'

'You do remember what I said about fighting and killing?'

'I'm sure that greedy Armstrong can be reasoned with. Once we arrive we'll set him straight. That'll be the end of it.'

'All right, Sparky.' Travis gave in. 'So long as you don't think there will be any real trouble.'

'Hannah would have told me if she wanted me to bring along a couple hardcase sorts. I suspect we'll be kicking off our boots and enjoying the sun in the evening before the summer's gone.'

With a few dollars back pay and the clothes on their backs, Travis resigned his commission, Sparky mustered out, and the two of them headed for Colorado.

CHAPTER THREE

By June of 1869, Rowena had become the mistress of Buckeye's house. She made the decisions and did most of the work. Buckeye had grown more crippled from his 'ruematiz' every year and couldn't get around without the use of a cane. Life had often been hard with him, but he had never raised a hand or his voice to Rowena. He had taught her how to survive and they had gotten by.

As his crippling grew worse she had begun to take care of him and provide for their livelihood. She planted a small garden, set traps and snares for game, cleaned and cooked the edible critters, and then processed the hides for selling. She also did the laundry and kept the wood bin full. When it came on to winter she did most of the cutting and stacking of wood to get them through. She worked and lived a mostly solitary life with Buckeye. They had been together since the impromptu adoption and she felt lucky to share her life with him.

However, Rowena was not a kid any more. Although slight of build from constant physical work and getting by on mostly meat, wild plants, roots, seeds and berries, it was impossible to fight Nature. She was beginning to look her age.

'Walt asked about you again,' Buckeye said, after supper one night. 'You are comin' on to womanhood, Squirrel (seven years together and he never had called her Rowena). 'He offered me twenty dollars cash money and a beef critter for you yesterday. I was sorely tempted to take him up on it.'

'And who would you get to cook and clean for you? Who would move your traps and scrape and tan the hides? Who would cut wood so you could fire the stove and not freeze come winter?'

Buckeye tried to stand up – he appeared determined to make a special point of something – but couldn't get out of the chair. He sagged back down and heaved a sigh.

'I ain't wanting to have you worrying about me, Squirrel.' He grunted at his own words. 'Not that you would be real concerned no how, 'cause it ain't like I'm your real pa or nothing. But I've been feeling a tightness about my chest, and twice I've been struck with a sudden pain that steals my wind and doubles me over. I don't think I'll be around much longer.'

Rowena was immediately concerned. Buckeye was right; he was not her father, but he had taken her in like family. True, he had lied to the army about having a sickly wife, and she more than earned her keep, but the man was still her . . . well, her guardian.

'Why haven't you said something?' she demanded to know. 'We ought to get to a nearby town and have a doctor take a look at you.'

'I've had me sixty-four years on this here earth, hard-living years, for the most part, Squirrel. You think I want some book-read quack poking and prodding me, so he can inform me that I'm getting old? I'm only telling you, because I want you to be settled and taken care of.'

'Well, you can't get shed of me with a slimy maggot like Walt Pockman. He looks at me with lust in his eyes and makes my skin crawl whenever he's around.'

Buckeye showed a rare compassion. 'I don't want to worry about you after I'm gone. That's all.'

'I can take care of myself,' she declared. 'I can keep on doing what I've been doing for you. I've learned how to ready the hides and pelts, and I know what they're worth. I'm also better than you at fishing and finding the best places for a trap or snare. You admitted you never caught more than a couple rabbits all the time you was working these hills alone. Once I took over the chore, we had all we wanted.'

'Yeah, you're as natural a hunter as a coyote, but most of the game is played out around here, and we've done spent most of the money we saved from buffalo hunting. Besides, this ain't no life for a woman. Don't you want to have a man to love and a family of your own some day?'

Rowena ducked her head. 'I was an Indian captive, you remember. A good many people will think of me as a squaw . . . or worse.'

'Buffalo chips, gal! You were a young girl back then, not yet thirteen years of age.'

'That didn't save a good many others my age.'

'Look. You don't have to say nothing about those few months as a hostage. I took you in when you were orphaned. That's all you need to tell anyone.'

'But it would be easier if I was to marry Walt, because he already knows. Isn't that what you're trying to say?'

'We was passing the jug back and forth,' Buckeye whined defensively. 'He asked how I ended up with you. It just kind of slipped out.'

'Well, you can bet the winter store of wood, I'll spend my life as a hermit or go back to skinning buffalo, before I consent to hitch up with Walt.'

Buckeye maintained a long stare at her, as if

willing her to change her mind. When she held fast and did not break eye contact, a slight grin came to his lips.

'Can't be around someone like me and not pick up a few of my personal traits. I reckon you've got a mind of your own.'

'Yes, Buckeye. If nothing else, tending chores and watching over you these past few years has taught me how to survive.'

'All right, Squirrel, I'll tell Walt the answer is no. He won't like it, but you ought to have a chance to find your own man.' He chuckled. 'I doubt you will choose anyone like me.'

Rowena laughed. 'I think of you as my very unusual uncle, Buckeye. I know you ain't crazy, but it don't stop folks from saying it's so. And you're right, if I ever fall in love with a man, he's not likely to be an over-the-hill Indian scout and buffalo hunter.'

The first time Neville Pockman realized his brother had a flame burning for Buckeye's girl was after Walt spied on her while she was washing at a stream. He came into their cabin looking flush and wild-eyed, full of excitement and unable to hide the fires of passion that consumed his mind and body.

'I tell you, Nat,' he barely contained his enthusiasm, 'she was wearing a long shirt, but it didn't hide her legs below the knees. And when she happened to splash some water on that there shirt. . . .' He practically howled at the sky and clapped his hands. 'I mean the material clung to her enough that I could see she's a full-growed woman. She sure ain't the little girl Buckeye calls Squirrel, not no more.'

'Dag-nabit, Walt,' Neville tried to calm him down. 'You can't go getting all heated up for that there woman. She thinks we're a couple no-good beggars and avoids us both like we was rabid dogs. You ain't got a chance of courting her.'

Walt was not dissuaded. 'Look here, Nat, we could use someone to run the household and do a few chores. You've seen the amount of work Buckeye gets out of that little gal. She ought to be eager to join up with us. It would lessen her work load by a bunch. There's only the three of us and Waco is often off by himself.'

'That man has some demons,' Neville said, speaking of their one hired hand. 'I'll bet he don't sleep more than two or three hours at night.'

'What do you expect?' Walt said. 'He was at Vicksburg. He was wounded twice and lost both of his brothers and his uncle in one day. If he hadn't gotten drunk with us that time at Breckenridge, we wouldn't have known a thing about it. He's got it bottled up inside and it eats at him every day. I'm guessing, if it was me I would never sleep right again either.'

31

Neville got back to the present situation. 'So what if Squirrel has her mind set on finding someone else?'

'Who's she gonna find better'n me? And way out here, to boot!'

Neville held up his hands to keep Walt from losing his temper. 'I'm just saying, she don't look on us with any favor. You can't just drag her over here by the hair and chain her to the cook stove.'

Walt didn't seem to hear the argument. 'No cutting wood, and no more traps or skinning and tanning hides. She wouldn't have to do the hunting, trapping or fishing to put food on the table. I tell you, Nat, she ought to jump at the chance to become my wife.'

'That's true enough, but you can't count on her saying yes.'

'Ain't no one else going to ask her,' Walt was sarcastic. 'She was a prisoner of the Sioux for several months. You know what them bucks did to the women they captured.'

'You told me that Buckeye claimed she was never touched, that he said she pretended to be out of her mind and they left her alone.'

Walt scoffed. 'Buckeye would say anything to protect her. He don't want to give up his nurse, cook, and keeper.'

'That's another problem with getting the gal for

your own, Walt. She's Buckeye's personal slave and takes care of him. No way he's gonna want to give her up.'

A dark cloud seemed to pass across Walt's face. 'Rowena is going to belong to me, Nat. I don't care what it takes. It's going to happen.'

'If you say so, big brother,' Neville gave in. 'You've always had a knack for getting what you wanted. I suspect you'll get her in the end.'

'I've been patient long enough. I'm going to bring that gal home and make her my wife. Once she's hitched to me, she will learn to do whatever I say.'

'You know me, I'll follow your lead,' Neville said. 'However you want to play this, you can deal me in.'

Walt smiled broadly and patted him on the shoulder. 'I know I can always count on you. This will work out fine. You'll see.'

'Well, Capt'n,' Sparky spoke to Travis. 'That's the last of the herd. Another few weeks to finish the branding and it's money in the bank. The Nalens will be out of debt to the bank and we'll have ourselves a fair chunk of change too.'

'I got confirmation from the quartermaster at the fort. He said the army would pay us on delivery, and they'll take every last steer. Once we ship them from the railhead we only have to sit back and relax until we get payment.'

Hayes rode over from where he had been closing the gate. 'Whatta' you think, Sparky,' he wanted to know, 'few more days with the branding-iron, then we fatten them up for a couple weeks?'

'Might take a little longer than that, pard. We'll push them on to the south pasture and let them eat along the creek. We want to pack on the pounds before we get started. Every pound on the hoof is another thirty cents in profit.'

'I'll tell Riley. Me and him ain't been to a big city in more than four years. We aim to tie a sign around our necks that reads: "If you see us sober, get us another drink!" '

'Good thing my brother-in-law isn't going,' Sparky teased back. 'He would likely have you locked up the first night we hit town and not let you out until we were ready to head for home.'

'Sure enough, your sister has made him a domesticated man.'

The two continued to josh one another while Travis took a final count of the herd. He had learned the trade and worked hard to earn his keep. Four years on the place and, even being the youngest, he was promoted to ranch foreman.

As for the problem with their neighbors, the Diamond A Ranch had not given them any problems lately. Once Sparky and he had arrived, the boundary dispute was quickly settled. There were still the occasional taunts or bad-mouthing from some of their riders, but Travis had never let it get out of hand. Considering that Sparky's brother-in-law, Abe Nalen, and both of the other hands were over fifty years old, it prevented the kind of brawling in which younger men might have engaged.

Hannah was in the yard when Travis rode up. She was always friendly and smiling around Travis, likening him to the son she had never had. They had raised three girls, but all had married and moved away.

'I've got some cookies in the oven,' she said in greeting. 'They should be ready in a few minutes.'

'Reckon I can stick around long enough for a treat like that,' he replied. 'Just finished the final tally for Abe.'

Hannah wiped her hands on her apron as Travis stepped down from the back of his horse. He wrapped the reins around a hitching post and saw the woman had her motherly expression on her face.

'Mrs Hanley mentioned her daughter was coming for a visit. You remember I told you she has been attending a school for higher learning in Denver?'

'Yes, she wants to be a teacher or something . . . right?'

'She hopes to end up teaching at one of the women's colleges back East.'

'Sounds ambitious.'

'She isn't being courted by anyone at the moment.'

Travis laughed. 'I don't think I'd be much of a suitor for a lady like that, Mrs Nalen. I barely learned to read and write.'

'You were an officer in the war,' she argued.

'Only because I was about the last man standing,' Travis quipped. 'I had a tough time when it came to writing reports or letters. I'm not the scholarly type.'

'There aren't many choices around here,' Hannah said. 'I'd have loved for you to meet my daughters, back when they were dating age. You don't know how lonely it is for me, surrounded by three old bachelors and my husband. I'd like to see you with a girl of your own.'

'Yeah, I've got so much to offer.'

'Abe said he would help to build you a house, over near the creek, so you wouldn't have to carry water too far. You are our foreman and Abe says, after this sale, he is going to make you a partner. It's the only way we will be able to live here once he retires. We need someone younger to manage the ranch.'

'I appreciate the partnership and your worrying

about me, Mrs Nalen, but there are only a few single girls around and they all have their pick of suitors.'

'You're as good a catch as any in the valley.'

'Yes, but I'm not looking for just any girl.' Travis grinned. 'I'm waiting until I find one like you.'

Hannah laughed at the flattery. 'You just earned an extra cookie. I'll have them on a plate by the time you finish talking business with Abe.'

Rowena checked the traps and snares, but the game was mostly played out within walking distance from the cabin. When they had first moved into the old trapper's shack Buckeye had been physically fit enough to take her camping for a few days at a time, to places where the game was plentiful. But now he was limited in what he could do. It took him a full five minutes to get out of bed and he relied heavily on a wooden cane he had fashioned whenever he left the house. He had seemed invincible when he claimed her at Camp Release, but age and his rugged lifestyle had taken its toll. This latest complaint about chest pains was especially worrisome. He might suffer apoplexy or a heart attack and die. Where would that leave her?

She went by the corral and checked the water for Burner, the pack-animal. Their only riding-horse had died during the last winter and Burner was all they had left. He was a ten-year-old mule, stubborn most of the time, and didn't neck-rein worth a hoot. Whenever they took him out they had to lead him on a rope or he would fight every step of the way.

Lost in her reverie, she didn't noticed a horse standing back in the brush until she was nearly to the cabin. Odd; whoever had ridden the animal had not used the hitching post out front. Rowena heard some muffled noises coming from inside and hurried to the half-open front door. She stopped dead, stunned at the sight!

Walt was sitting astraddle Buckeye's chest, his knees pinning Buckeye's arms, while he pressed a pillow to his face. Buckeye appeared to have ceased his struggling, his hands lay limp at his sides as Rowena flew into the room.

Snatching up the only weapon at hand – the knife she used for skinning critters or cutting rope – she charged at Walt.

He heard her coming and threw up his hands to prevent her from sticking him with the knife.

'Stop it, you silly heifer!' Walt cried. He twisted about, trying to catch hold of her wrist so he could take the knife away from Rowena. But he was trapped atop of Buckeye, unable to dismount from his position, and lacking the leverage for warding off an attack.

Rowena adroitly rotated the knife's direction and plunged it a second time.

Walt missed a frantic grab for her wrist and the blade sank deep in his chest. His eyes grew wide, his mouth gaped; he tumbled from his position and fell to the floor.

Rowena ignored him, tearing the pillow away from Buckeye's face, desperate to save him. But his mouth hung open, exposing his few remaining teeth and there was blood from his having bitten his tongue. The sightless eyes were wide open and staring blindly, revealing no sign of life. Buckeye was dead.

'Walt!' Neville's voice called from outside. 'Hey, big brother! You still in there? I couldn't locate the gal. She might be on her way back here.'

Rowena shoved the knife into her pocket, then pounced on Walt's inert body and yanked the gun from his holster. She moved quickly behind the door and stood out of sight. When Neville entered, she struck him along the back of his head with the barrel of the gun. He groaned and was knocked to the floor. Before he could recover, Rowena grabbed up her jacket and the small pouch of money she and Buckeye kept hidden next to the coffee pot. She raced outside, grabbed up the horse Neville had left standing at the hitching post and swung aboard. To slow the pursuit, she rode over and released Walt's horse. She fired off a shot and the steed bolted off in the direction of the Pockman ranch.

With no idea of where she was going, Rowena kicked Neville's horse into a lope and headed out of the hills. When she struck the main trail, she turned the animal and dug in her heels. There was no law within a hundred miles and she had not a single friend. Even the man who ran the trading post resented the fact that she never let him cheat Buckeye on prices. Buckeye had been a loner and Rowena had been satisfied to live a solitary existence. That lifestyle was gone now and she was on her own. Her only chance was to get away; get away and hide, because Neville would never stop hunting her. That man worshiped Walt; she had to run or die.

CHAPTER FOUR

The last few years of hard work were going to pay off at last. It was less than ten miles to the railhead now. They would load the hundred head of steers on to railcars and then wait until the money arrived from the army's paymaster. The estimated $3,000 was going to put the ranch on solid ground for another two or three years.

Travis cut off a wayward steer and hazed him back with the rest. He was hot, dusty, tired and felt as if he might never walk normal again, after so many long days in the saddle. But this was it, the payday they had been working for.

Riley rode over and coughed from the dust. 'Figure we ought to hold up for the night at the clearing ahead. Vogel should be back with some supplies from town by then.'

'If he don't give out before his horse. Sparky has

been complaining every mile about his aches and pains. Good thing this isn't a long trail drive.'

'He's always been a complainer,' Riley said, his voice revealing his fondness for the elder statesman of the ranch. 'Thing is, he is always the first man up in the morning and does more work than anyone else.'

'He was like that during the war too. Never stopped griping, yet volunteered for every job that came along.'

'Me and Hayes couldn't believe it when he joined up. First off, he tells us we're too old to fight a war, then he sneaks out in the middle of the night and enlists. That's Vogel for you, full of surprises.'

Travis chuckled, 'He's one of a kind all right. There was this one time—'

The sudden jolt cut off his sentence and knocked Travis out of the saddle. Dazed by the fall, he thought he heard the sound of distant gunfire. There came several more shots as he lay flat on his back and gasped for air. Blinded by the sun, he couldn't get his brain to function. He closed his eyes against the bright sky and listened to some men calling back and forth. A few moments passed – it could have been an hour or ten seconds – he didn't know which. Then the voices came in range of his hearing.

'You get the third man?' a nearby man called out.

'He's done!' came the answer. 'I done nailed him good.'

'We got the other two,' the first man shouted again. 'The herd is ours!'

Travis tried mightily, but he couldn't hold on to his awareness. It was lost to the dark void that rushed in to smother all sensation. Even fear for his two companions wasn't enough to keep him from lapsing into unconsciousness.

Bits of dreams came and went, a burning heat consuming Travis's body as he battled to rise to a sentient state. It seemed he was trapped in a limbo between life and death for days on end. At last a grating voice broke through the wall of silence.

'So help me, Capt'n, I'm gonna leave you here for the coyotes. I ain't no nursemaid. If'n you don't open your blinkers and show signs of life, I'm heading for the nearest saloon and order me some snake juice. I'll drink until I can't see straight.'

Travis attempted to penetrate the darkness and speak, but the words came out as a muffled groan.

'What's that?' Sparky's gruff voice came back. 'You trying to tell me you intend to live after all?' There came a sigh of relief. 'All right, Capt'n, I'll give you another five minutes.'

Travis felt a moisture against his lips and swallowed a few sips of water. He managed to open his eyes to tiny slits, but saw only blackness.

'Am I . . .' he had to swallow to regain his voice. 'Am I blind?'

'No more'n me,' Sparky said. 'It's the middle of the night, there's clouds hiding the moon, and I ain't advertising we're still alive by starting a fire.'

Travis began to feel sensations again. That wasn't all good. His entire left side began to throb, each beat of his heart causing a secondary spasm of pain to shoot through his upper body.

'H-how bad?' he managed to ask between waves of agony.

'I think the bullet missed your lungs and heart,' Sparky replied. 'Don't know how, but you are still alive . . . more or less. Lucky for you I watched a few of those army doctors work on wounded soldiers after a battle or two. I cleaned and stuffed up the holes you have in your back and chest.'

'Riley and Hayes?'

A sadness entered his friend's voice. 'Both dead. I give them a proper burial yesterday and said some final words over their bodies.'

'Damn it all, Sparky!' Travis moaned, suffering with the weight of the news. 'We didn't see this coming. They ambushed us and we didn't even put up a fight.'

'Cold-blooded killers, them rustling varmints,' Sparky said. 'Shot every one of you in the back. The cowards took no chances on any kind of fight.'

Travis's brain was muddled by the pain from his injuries, but he reasoned out the present situation. 'Looks like I owe you my life, Sparky.'

'You can buy me a couple drinks when we reach town and we'll call it even.'

'Sounds about right,' Travis replied. 'Although I don't feel as if my life is worth more than one beer at the moment.'

'At least I found your favorite hat. Good thing none of those back shooters seen the silver band, else they'd have stolen that too.'

'Do you think I ought still to consider the hat to be lucky?'

'You're the only one left alive,' Sparky remarked. 'Give credit to your hat or the Man Upstairs.'

'Think I'll say a thank-you prayer before I go back to sleep.'

'Yeah, but keep the hat too.'

Travis tried to grin but the pain and loss were too great. He closed his eyes.

'Get a little more sleep,' Sparky encouraged. 'There might be some rain in those clouds moving in. We need to get to town before the storm hits. No shelter out here in the open, less'n we crawl into a hole beneath a sagebrush.'

'My horse?'

'Them rustlers was only interested in the herd. I caught up two horses. One of them is yours and the

45

other belonged to Hayes. Riley's must have followed along with the herd.'

'Good thing you were in town buying grub. Otherwise we'd all be food for the coyotes and buzzards.'

'When I found you I thought you were dead. I about had you planted afore I noticed you were still breathing. Lucky for you I used my medical know-ledge and took time to look, else you would have woken up under several feet of dirt.'

'Did you get a look at the men who attacked us?'

'Sorry, Capt'n, but I was too far away. I heard the echo of several shots, but by the time I found you and the others, the killers and the herd was gone. There was dust up the trail a piece, but I wasn't of a mind to tackle them alone. Soon as I discovered you weren't dead I stuck here and did what mending I could.'

Travis sighed and fell silent. Allowing his eyes to close cost him his consciousness right away. He hoped the new day would bring him enough strength to ride. Riley and Hayes never hurt a soul, and now they were dead, murdered by several back-shooting snakes. He would sleep, but he would not rest, not until they found out who those ruthless killers were and brought them to justice!

Rowena moved like a ghost, quietly placing each

foot on the soft earth. The family living here had a dog, but it often slept inside the house. If the mutt heard her digging in the garden he might set up a racket or come charging out at her.

She hung the two skinned rabbits on the clothes' line, then proceeded to pick a few carrots, a small head of lettuce and two ripe tomatoes. Sticking the vegetables into the cloth bag she carried, she quietly retreated to the trail and made her way through the darkness.

Rowena had good night vision. She carried Walt's Navy Colt in one hand and her bag of goods in the other. There were a few dangers around, mostly snakes, coyotes or the occasional puma. Most predators didn't bother a grown person, but she had encountered a bear once that didn't run from her. She had backed away slowly and went around him, fearful that he might charge at any moment. Thankfully, he had been going somewhere at the time and merely remained watchful of her maneuver. Other than animals, the single true danger she avoided was people.

Once she'd crossed the creek she made her way up to her shelter in the rocks. She could smell the coming rain and hurried as quickly as she dared. A sharp rock stung her right heel and reminded her that she would have to do something about her footgear. She had made a pair of moccasins, but the soles were wearing very thin. Most of the animals she trapped or killed were small and did not have a thick enough hide for decent shoe leather. Her moccasins had been fashioned from a freshly killed deer she had found some weeks back. Obviously shot by a hunter, it had escaped his clutches and then died where it had lain down. She remembered that day as if it had been her birthday. She had dried some of the meat for jerky and used the hide for her bed and the much-needed footwear. Thinking of the venison roast and steak she had cooked caused her stomach to rumble and her mouth to water. Squirrels, rabbits and sage hens were the bulk of her meat diet, along with the occasional eggs she would find or trade for.

Using snares, traps and mostly rocks for weapons, she saved the precious ammunition in her pistol. Plus, Buckeye had shown her how to shoot, but that had been with his old rifle. One shot had left her shoulder bruised and sore for a week. She had kept Walt's pistol, but she had been forced to put Neville's horse out of its misery when it broke a leg crossing a prairie-dog village, and there had been the shot she fired at Buckeye's cabin to run off Walt's horse. It left her with only three bullets.

The gun was for an emergency, as she had learned enough from Buckeye about fishing and using traps to keep from starving. Also, a single shot might give her away to some wandering farmer or cowpoke. All of her care to keep hidden would be wasted if she dared fire at an animal and was then discovered.

The steep slope became littered with an outcrop of rocks, the craggy surface only a few feet below her private den. She had discovered it by accident and converted it to a home. Fashioning a cover for the opening had been a major chore, but she had found a discarded army blanket and hooked it into place with some old wire. She hoped it would deter a mountain lion or bear from entering the small cavern. To this point in time, she had been undisturbed by any animals.

She kept the gun ready as she moved the blanket aside. There appeared to be no uninvited visitors in the den so she entered quickly. She didn't light a candle, but swept a hand over her bedding, making certain no insects had taken up residence. She possessed but two nearly spent candles – salvaged from an abandoned pilgrim's handcart – and a few precious matches. She saved those for any emergency that might come up. As for her cooking or heat, she used an old coffee pot to hold hot ashes and coals during the night so she could start a small, smokeless fire each morning.

Rowena sagged down on to her makeshift bed and used a single quilt for a cover. Once stretched out, she thought how she could best use the vegetables so as not to let anything go to waste. She hated having to resort to stealing (though she always left hides or meat as payment), but it was necessary to have a variety in her food. She did worry what would happen come winter. She'd been living in the hills for several weeks and had avoided being seen. One time, however, when she had been fishing the stream, a couple of kids had come near and went for a swim. Quickly ducking behind a bush, she listened to them talking back and forth. They mentioned a rumor about a renegade Indian who was hiding out in the hills. The two young people laughed at how the Indian had taken their grandmother's bonnet and left her some wild flowers and a small sack of ripe currants. The one acknowledged that he loved the currant pie his mother had made from the berries.

A smile played along her lips. *So I'm a renegade Indian, a refugee from one of the reservations!* It was a good cover story and, by always trading something for what she took, no one seemed anxious to catch the culprit. If she had simply stolen goods or articles, the farmers might have gotten together and searched for her. Or they might have hired someone to track her down.

Rowena yawned and snuggled under the blanket. She would need to wash her clothes and blanket at the creek pretty soon. Nothing stayed clean for very long in the small cave. And she had real concerns about how she would survive and stay warm when the snows came. However, there was no need to fret about it, not for another few weeks until the cold weather hit. If she could get a needle and thread, she would try and make a robe from rabbit hides. She had no money left, having spent what little she had during her travels to escape. However, she could try and trade something at the general store. It would be risky to enter town, but she needed salt, flour and a few other things. She dismissed her worries for the time being. With delicious thoughts of how to best enjoy her fresh vegetables, she drifted off to sleep.

There was only the town barber who acted as a peace officer when one was needed. He was past his prime and no longer rode a horse. When Sparky brought him to speak to Travis, the man was sympathetic, but offered no help. Yes, he had seen the herd of cattle pass by, but they were some distance off of the main trail, likely going to the railhead. The men driving the herd never entered town and no one spoke to any of them. To his recollection, there had appeared to be three or four men in the group, pushing about a hundred head of cattle.

Travis and Sparky got a meal at Millie's Eats for

fifty cents each, then they spent the day in the hay loft at the blacksmith's place. It rained on and off until sundown, then it was cool and calm for sleeping.

Travis was glad Sparky had been off getting supplies during the ambush. The older man had always been a storyteller, sharing tales with Travis all through the war, then doing much of the same while working at the Nalen ranch. He could talk about places from Mexico to Montana, from Oregon to New York. Whether he had actually been to all those places and done everything he claimed was doubtful, but he was a knowledgeable sort.

Shorter than Travis by three or four inches, Sparky was fairly stout for his five and a half feet. Since leaving the Union army, he had grown shaggy-looking. He hadn't shaved or cut his hair in a good many months. Professing to still be thirty-nine years old, he had gray sprinkled in his short, bushy beard, above his ears and even mixed into eyebrows, which looked like two large, fuzzy caterpillars.

Travis dreamed about their lost friends nearly every time he closed his eyes and the agony of their deaths weighed upon him each time he came awake. With a grim determination, he knew what he had to do. As soon as he could move around, he would begin working to get back his strength. Sparky and he had to try and get justice for the murders of Riley and Hayes before they returned home.

Home: it had quickly become a place of dim prospects. Without the cash for selling the cattle, the ranch would be in dire need. The money they were supposed to make on the beef would have paid all of the Nalen debts and had plenty left over. Now it would be difficult for the small ranch even to survive.

Neville Pockman held the man by the throat, so angry he could barely contain himself. He fought to regain control of his passions. He had to get information out of this man and would do what it took to get answers.

'Where'd you drop her off?' He snarled the question. 'Tell me, or I'll wring your neck like a chicken!'

'Easy, Neville,' Waco tried to soothe his ire from a step back of him.

Neville lessened his grip, but continued to scowl at the stage guard.

'Paddy is the one who let her ride in the coach,' the man whined. 'We didn't have any passengers, so he allowed she could ride to the next stop for two-bits.'

'Then she got off at Grand Forks?'

'That's as far as we took her. After that I never saw her again.'

'What about the driver?'

'I dunno. I think Paddy said something about her catching a ride with some farmer, one of them who had come in for supplies. I got no idea which way she went or who she was with.'

'But it was a farmer, huh?'

'There's ranches and farms scattered all the way from the Utah border clean up to Denver, mister. It could have been a clodhopper from ten or a hundred miles away. There ain't no way of knowing.'

'He's got no reason to lie to us, Neville,' Waco said, patting him on the shoulder.

Neville let go of the man and swore. 'I won't rest until I settle the hash of that sneaky little witch.'

'I've told you all I know, boys,' the man vowed. 'I'd sure help if I could.'

Neville swallowed his ire and began to think rationally. He didn't want this joker calling some law dog down on him for getting rough. In an effort to quell the man's fear and possibly win his understanding, he sorrowfully lowered his head.

'She smothered a poor old trapper named Buckeye with a pillow and robbed him of everything he owned,' he lied. 'When my brother showed up, she stabbed and killed him. I didn't know anything was wrong until she clubbed me from behind and stole my horse. She sure 'nuff figured me for dead.'

He snorted in contempt. 'But that was her big mistake. Waco here found me and saved my life.'

'Sounds like a real bad female,' the driver sympathized.

'Yes, well, there's no way she expected us to track her this far. I'd wager she thinks she's free and rid of us by this time.' He peered at the man, trying to tell if the story was sinking in. 'As for my horse, the silly cow ran my gelding near to death and didn't have the smarts to rest or take proper care of the poor critter. We found where she went through some bad country and my fine little horse busted its leg. She done kilt it and left it there for the coyotes to chew on.'

'The murdering, thieving little tart.' The man grated the words, showing support for Neville's position. 'If Paddy and me had known, we'd have seen she was locked up.'

'I'm sorry for getting rough with you,' Neville managed the apology with a Herculean effort. 'The gal has been a curse to me since we first set eyes on her. Buckeye was a gentle old hermit, taking care of the runt since she was kid. He was on his death bed and she up and killed him in the night. We stopped by to check on the poor man, and she stabs my brother and clubs me with a pistol. That gal is meaner than a wolverine.'

'She had a meek look about her that fooled us,'

the man admitted. 'I can understand your being hot to get even. Shucks, I'd sic you on her trail without blinking twice, but I honestly ain't got no idea where she went.'

Neville gave the man a grateful nod. 'Thanks, buddy. I'm about out of my head over this.'

'Well, good luck finding the little sidewinder.'

Neville said so-long and he and Waco walked away.

'Dad-blast the luck! All these weeks chasing her and that feisty vixen is likely hiding out somewhere, maybe fifty or a hundred miles from here.' Neville swore bitterly. 'Who'd have thought she could escape us all this time?'

'She knowed to run hard and fast,' Waco agreed. 'Still, she's a woman alone and that is gonna eventually be her downfall. We'll find her all right, and when we do. . . .' His hands closed into tight fists. 'She will pay the full price for killing Walt!'

CHAPTER FIVE

Sparky, by virtue of his claim to being able to do 'most everything, was able to find work for several days while Travis recovered his strength. A week after being shot, Travis was able to walk and move about gingerly. The two of them were having supper at the town eatery when Travis brought up the future.

'I think we can set out to track those cattle thieves tomorrow.'

'Going to be hard to find them. They've had enough time to sell the herd and leave the country.'

Travis said, 'They killed Riley and Hayes; they stole our herd. I can't go back to the Nalens with nothing.'

'I wired Abe and told him what happened, when we first got to town,' Sparky said. 'Abe replied back that he was sorry and didn't blame us.'

'Damn, Sparky, I feel like I did after that last battle of the war. It's hard to cope with the senseless death of good men. And this time I don't blame the politicians who should have found a peaceful way to settle their differences. This time I blame those dirty, filthy bushwhackers, and I won't rest until we find them.'

'I agree with the notion, Capt'n, but where do we start looking?'

Travis thought for a moment. 'They wouldn't sit around with a bunch of stolen cattle. Smart play would be to drive the beef to the nearest railhead and either ship or sell the herd.'

'I sent a telegram to the US marshal's office. Finally tracked him down at Silver Crest, Colorado. Remember how I told you how I wore a badge as a deputy for the marshal once or twice, way back before the war. I helped to clean up a couple towns and brought in a few unsavory villains. We have his support for our efforts to bring those killers in.' Sparky speared another chunk of meat from his plate. 'That will make this here chase more legal.'

'You mean one of the wild stories you told me was actually true?'

Sparky put on a hurt look. 'You cut me deep saying something like that, Capt'n. I never make up stories.' He lifted a shoulder in a half-shrug. 'I might add a slight embellishment from time to time, but I never tell an outright lie.'

'OK, I apologize for doubting you.'

'You can't unring a bell. I'm your best friend and I've got feelings. You shouldn't go and trod all over them.'

'Are you finished?' Travis asked drily. 'If this is a long sad song about betrayal and disappointment, I'll get another cup of coffee so I can stay awake.' With a sigh. 'Of course, it would only add to your woes if I fell asleep while you're complaining.'

'Fine,' Sparky snorted unhappily. 'I'm finished.'

'So we've got our plan for this campaign. We follow the trail of the herd until we learn enough about the rustlers to track them down.'

'Yes, sir, Capt'n. Be just like being back in the army. I'll tag along and make sure you don't do something stupid . . . like get yourself killed.'

Travis gave a nod. 'I intend to see those murderers either dead or behind bars.'

'Taking on the job of a peacemaker.' Sparky laughed. 'Good thing you've got me along. With my rather extensive experience, we'll do just fine.'

'You make me feel more optimistic already.'

'I've gotten to know the livery man pretty well since we took to camping in his loft. Gave him some pointers on improving his forge. Anyway, he said he'd make us a fair offer for our extra mount . . . unless you think we ought to keep a spare horse for packing supplies.'

'If we get hot on the trail of those rustlers we might need to have some supplies handy. I think we ought to keep him.'

'All right; we'll pool what money we have and buy enough chuck to get us started. We can trade the extra saddle for our keep at the barn.'

Travis said, 'Actually, I never spent much of the money I earned at the ranch. I've enough of a stake that we can get by for a time.'

'I begin to like our chances more, seeing's how we won't have to stop and work a day or two at a time while we're still doing our tracking.'

'Any idea where those rustlers will sell the herd?' Travis asked.

'I'll send off a few more telegraph messages. I know a good many people around this part of the country. I bet I can get a direction for us to start looking.'

'You got me a job with Nalen, you saved my life, and you know lawmen and telegraphers all over the country too. Sparky, I can't tell you how much you're worth as a friend.'

The gent laughed at his praise. 'And all the time we were together, fighting the war, you thought I was just another dog-face sergeant.'

Rowena entered town before daylight and found an

empty shed where she could wait for the general store to open. She had cleaned her buckskin skirt and the well-worn yellow blouse as best she could, put on her old shoes and done a thorough job of washing. Her hair was reasonably clean as well, with most of it tucked under the bonnet she wore. It was not a very fashionable outfit, but it was all she had.

Keylock was a fair-sized town. It had a general store and a boarding house that also offered baths and a barber. Plus there was a saloon with a bar and gambling tables, along with a stage, freight and mail office, which handled a little banking. Being on the main trail, people were constantly coming or going, some heading through Colorado, and others on to Utah or Kansas. Some herds of cattle also passed by on their way to a railhead or stock pens. With so many people passing through, Rowena hoped to blend in like one of the many travelers.

She counted herself lucky when it was the store-keeper's wife who opened the door to the general store. She had watched the woman's husband load a wagon earlier and leave town. He obviously made deliveries to nearby farms and would be gone for some time. Mrs Dillard critically eyed her tattered dress when she entered, but smiled. 'Good morning,' she said in greeting. 'You just get into town?'

Rowena managed a friendly demeanor. 'Yes, I

wonder if you could help me. My uncle gave me a few tanned hides, but I don't know where to take them for sell or trade.'

'Let's have a look, dear,' Mrs Dillard offered.

Rowena lifted her cloth carrying-bag and dumped the lot on the countertop – six rabbit furs, one fox hide and a skunk pelt. She gave the woman a helpless gesture.

'I don't know exactly how much these are worth around here. Could you possibly take these in exchange for a few items I need?'

Mrs Dillard picked up each of the hides, felt the fur and blew a little along the thick coat of the fox hide. She appeared experienced at such things and paused to do some calculating in her head.

'They would be worth more if you traded them at a tannery, but we don't have one local. Any hides we take in we have to send up the line to a buyer. It means we pay less than you might get somewhere else.'

'I understand.'

'Tell you what,' the woman said, 'If you are sure you want to trade them to me, I'll let you have three dollars' worth of goods for the bunch.'

Rowena's heart leapt. 'Oh, that sounds like a very fair price.'

A spark of pleasure entered the woman's eyes, as if she enjoyed seeing Rowena's delight over the offer. She said, 'You get what you need and we'll tally it up.'

Although she had a list in mind, Rowena took her time and studied each and every item she picked up. The needle and thread she chose had to be heavy duty enough to sew hides and she also wanted more matches and candles. She feared that buying salt, sugar and flour would perk the woman's curiosity, but she had to have those things.

Another customer entered the store, but Rowena was careful to not make eye contact. She continued to work out her purchases with great care and deliberation, waiting until she could again be alone with Mrs Dillard. Once the customer left she carried her bag to the counter. She had figured out the worth to the last cent.

'I wish I could afford to hire you to help around here,' Mrs Dillard remarked after totaling the goods. 'You managed to spend exactly three dollars. It's uncommon for a person to be able to add so many items up in their head and come out exact.'

Rowena blushed at the praise. 'I did some trading and handled money for my uncle. He was . . .' she corrected the statement at once, '*is* a cripple and I've been taking care of him for several years.'

'That dress you're wearing looks like something an Indian squaw might wear. It will take more than a needle and thread to make it presentable. Is that the only clothing you have?'

'I kind of ended up on my own for a spell,' Rowena admitted.

'My sister came to visit last fall and left one of her outfits behind. You're a mite thinner than her, but I'd like to get it out of my closet. You might be able to take it in enough to fit.'

Rowena was stunned by the offer but quickly accepted. 'That would be very helpful. A good many folks look at me like a beggar woman, wearing this ragged outfit.' She lifted her chin. 'And I swear, I've never begged or asked for nothing from anyone.'

Mrs Dillard disappeared through the back door of the store and returned moments later. The dress had been folded neatly for storage, but she shook it out so Rowena could see it. The pattern was plain, a dark brown in color, with a ruffle along the collar and with long sleeves. Being of a heavy material, it would be durable and well suited for the cold weather ahead.

'It's much too nice!' Rowena objected. 'I couldn't take something like that without being able to pay you.'

'Nonsense, honey.' Mrs Dillard dismissed her concern. 'You'll be helping me to clean out a spot I need for my own stuff. If you can use it, it's yours.'

Rowena accepted the dress graciously and stuck it into her bag. She thanked the woman again as she left the store. Her spirits soared at the success of her shopping expedition as she started down the walk with her sack full of treasure.

Suddenly her path was blocked by two men. One was fairly tall, with narrow-set eyes, while the other was lean and slobbered from a mouthful of tobacco. Both were dressed like cowboys.

'Wal now,' the tall one said, looking her up and down. 'Fix your blinkers on the filly here, Ponch.'

'By jingo, I see her, Tibbs,' the other replied. 'Dressed like a squaw, but she ain't Injun, not with them light-colored eyes.'

'Just a wandering ragamuffin, you think?'

Rowena backed up a step and tried to go around. Tibbs moved to prevent her from getting past.

'Stand easy, gal,' he said, showing his uneven teeth in a grin. 'We ain't the kind to break the spirit of a good horse.' With a chortle, 'We only break them to ride.'

'I'm not a horse,' she said tightly. 'Kindly get out of my way. I've got to meet up with my uncle.'

Her second attempt to pass was not successful either. This time it was Ponch who obstructed her path.

'What kind of man is your uncle that he would let you walk around looking like a half-mix between a white woman and either a Mexican or Indian?' Tibbs remarked.

'Yeah, sweetheart,' Ponch said with a leer. 'How's 'bout you join us for breakfast at Sadie's place?' He paused to spit a dark stream of juice on to the dusty street, then had to pause and wipe some dribble off his chin.

'You can't even spit tobacca proper,' Rowena dressed him down. 'My uncle could blind a snake with a stream of juice at fifteen feet and never break his stride.'

Ponch stared at her wide-eyed. 'The hell you say!'

'Best spitting man for a hundred miles around,' she bragged. 'And he has kilt more buffalo than you can count, some from more'n a half-mile off. If you two don't let me pass, he'll be using both of your hides for target practice!'

Ponch did move aside, but Tibbs reached out to grab hold of her wrist and stopped her.

'You wouldn't be funning us about your uncle, would you?'

'Let go!' Rowena snapped, and jerked her hand free. 'Buckeye will whale the daylights out of you both!'

Tibbs took a step toward her, as if prepared to drag her down the walk. But the door of the store opened and Mrs Dillard stormed out on to the walk. She lit into the pair of pesky cowboys like a mother grizzly protecting her cubs.

'You two stray dogs stop pestering my customers,

unless you want my Barney to give you a lesson in manners!' She put her hands on her hips and glared at the two men. 'I'm warning you, Tibbs.' She thrust out her jaw at him. 'I know you and Ponch are the ones who molested that young lady the other day.'

'Molested?' Tibbs objected to the term. 'She's the one who started swinging on us. I was only holding her wrists to stop her from hitting us.'

'You about broke her arm!' Mrs Dillard shot back. 'Now both of you git! Or I'll tell Barney to lock you both up for a few days. Maybe then you'd behave yourselves.'

'Hey! Take it easy, Sue,' Tibbs said. 'You don't have to threaten us. We was only asking the lady if she wanted to join us for breakfast.'

'Don't you be calling me by my first name, Tibbs,' she said testily. 'You aren't someone I consider to be all that sociable with.'

The two men lifted their hands as if she had pointed a gun at them. 'Cripes, you've got a short fuse in the mornings.' Tibbs shook his head. 'No wonder Barney leaves at daylight with deliveries.'

Ponch guffawed and winked at Tibbs. 'That's the truth. Betcha he gets out of her path until she first has time to gnaw on a bone or eat some raw meat.'

'Git!' Mrs Dillard shouted again.

The two men rotated about and shuffled off

down the street. As soon as they were out of earshot, Rowena turned back to the store owner's wife.

'I'm sorry,' she said softly. 'I didn't mean to cause no trouble.'

There was a shrewd look in the woman's eyes. 'I ain't the nosy type, so I won't ask about your situation,' she said, her voice hushed so the words wouldn't carry. 'But I'm no fool. I believe you're the one who is living back in the hills. Some of the farmer's wives have spoken about you.'

Rowena gasped in shock, neither admitting or denying the assumption.

Mrs Dillard dismissed her shock with a sympathetic expression. 'I've known a few women who were forced to escape bad circumstances, so I don't pass judgment. What I am saying is, no one else knows the phantom who comes during the night and trades for what they take is a female. Now, I'm not going to tell anyone either, but I can't see how you're going to survive all on your own.'

'I-I don't know what to say, Mrs Dillard.'

'You can call me Sue,' she offered. Then, without waiting for Rowena to respond, 'If you're wanted by the law or something, you would do well to get it sorted out proper. My Barney is the acting town sheriff when one is needed. He might be able to help.'

'I'm . . . Rowena,' she murmured only her first

name, 'and I don't know if the law is looking for me or not. I do know a very bad man is searching for me, and he won't be alone.'

A sadness clouded Sue's face. 'Then there isn't anything I can do for you.' It was a statement. 'I'm sorry.'

'You've been very helpful,' Rowena told her. 'You done allowed me a very fair price on the pelts and you gave me a wonderful new dress. Besides that, you stuck up for me when those two cowboys started to bother me. I'm beholden to you.'

'All right,' Sue accepted the thanks with humility. 'But things can be hard on your own. If you need to trade for food or supplies again, you come see me. I'll do what I can for you.'

'You're a very kind lady.'

Sue frowned. 'You aren't thinking of spending the winter out there, living like an animal?'

'I'm not certain how long it will be until it's safe.' Rowena took a deep breath. 'The man who's looking for me won't stop, not for a long time.'

'You're sure Barney can't help?'

'Being a lawman, your husband might be on the other side.'

Sue had to move as a young couple and their two children passed by to enter the store. She had no more time.

'All right, dear. I'll just say good luck to you, and

don't hesitate to come again if you need something.'

Rowena displayed a warmth of appreciation when she spoke. 'Thank you, Sue. I mean it. Thank you very much.'

CHAPTER SIX

Tibbs nudged Ponch with his elbow. Instead of breakfast, they were standing by the bakery deciding whether they wanted to buy a pastry before heading back to their ranch.

'See there?' he said, tipping his head in the direction Rowena had taken. 'That gal went down the alley. What do you bet she don't show up in town for another month or so?'

Ponch rubbed the brittle stubble along his chin. 'Yeah, she's no ordinary sort, dressed like she is.'

'I've been keeping watch since we arrived. There ain't no new wagons on the street or camped outside of town, so she didn't come in with some wandering pilgrims or farmers passing through.'

'What about that uncle of hers? He might have pitched a camp yonder somewhere.'

Tibbs snorted his contempt. 'If he exists at all, I'll

71

bet he's nowhere close.'

'So, what's your thinking?'

'Remember the stories we've heard about the Indian living out in the hills, the one no one has seen or been able to catch?'

'What of it?'

Tibbs wondered why he tried. Sometimes, when he looked into Ponch's eyes, it was like two dark windows in an empty house; no one was home.

'The gal's shoes were worn through and that buckskin skirt looks like something a squaw would wear. As for the top, it's got more patches and holes than a mended fence. I'll bet she's the one who's been doing the stealing around the valley.'

Ponch laughed. 'You're on the wrong stage, pard. Why would a woman want to live like a wild Indian?'

'If my horse wasn't getting new shoes, we would sure enough get after her and take a look.'

Ponch put on a serious look. 'You mean it? You really think she is the one doing the stealing and trading?'

'I overheard a couple of farmer hags talking at the store a couple days back. One said how the thief had taken a bonnet but left enough fresh berries for a pie. What kind of Indian is going to do that?'

'That's for certain true. I never seen no Indian – buck or squaw – wearing a bonnet. And any red-hide brave would sure enough keep them berries for his own self.'

'Soon as we break those last two mustangs and get them sold, we'll take us a coupla days and go scout around for the girl. If she don't want to be seen around town and is hiding out in the hills, there must someone looking for her. I'm betting she'll treat us real nice to keep from being turned over to whoever it is.'

'Treat us nice? You mean she might fix us a meal or something?'

Tibbs wasn't sure if the man was joking. He punched him lightly on the shoulder. 'Yeah, *or something.*'

Ponch emitted a raucous chortle. It was his odd kind of laughter, when he didn't really know if he had gotten the joke or if there was even a joke being told. Tibbs knew the man's brain was usually on holiday, except, possibly, for the second Tuesday of each week, but he was as loyal as a hound and never complained.

The two of them had been together since the war. He had found Ponch wandering in a daze across a smoky battlefield, suffering from a head wound. Tibbs didn't know if he had been any smarter before being wounded or not. Most of Ponch's outfit had been killed, so he never met anyone in his unit to ask. It didn't really matter; they got along better than most brothers. That was mostly due to

Ponch letting Tibbs lead and he followed. Their ranch was a shack with a single corral. They owned a dozen cattle, which they had bought from some disreputable characters and quickly altered the brand. They also broke a few mustangs that they managed to catch, and did other jobs that came along. So far, they hadn't gotten rich, but they had gotten by.

Tibbs wondered if the ragged woman had a price on her head. There had to be a reason she was in hiding. Find the reason and there was a good chance someone would be willing to pay to get her back.

'You think of something funny?' Ponch asked, noticing the smirk on Tibbs's face.

Tibbs swatted the bigger man playfully. 'I was looking at your face – it always makes me laugh.'

Ponch howled with amusement. 'Yeah . . . makes me laugh sometimes too. Ma used to say if I was any homelier, she would have planted me knee deep and used me for a fence post.'

'I guess neither of us would win a handsome man contest.'

'Better to have brains than good looks, huh, pard?'

'That's the truth, my friend,' Tibbs replied. 'Yes sir, that's the truth.'

*

The four rustlers had been to the rail head and sold their stock at a huge discount to a local dealer. When Travis and Sparky confronted the buyer, the man was forthcoming. He'd never seen the four men before. They offered the herd for a cheap price, so they didn't have to wait for their money. The beef were branded but it took only a few days to alter them with a running iron and ship the cattle as his own.

'You know a brand has to be registered these days,' he informed Travis defensively. 'Driving stock without a brand or with that simple design you people were using is an invitation to rustlers.'

'Those men shot and killed two of our riders and left me for dead,' Travis told him icily. 'You bought stolen cattle from a bunch of murdering rustlers.'

'It ain't my fault!' the buyer cried. 'They claimed the critters belonged to them. I didn't have time to run a check on the brand to see if they were the real owners. I had a slaughterhouse waiting for beef.'

'You best think hard,' Travis warned the buyer. 'I want a complete description of each and every one of those men. You want to remain standing upright and enjoy eating solid food, you'd best tell me what kind of horses they were riding and any special features on either the men or the animals.'

The fellow didn't hesitate. He gave Travis and Sparky a good description of the four killers. Jubal

Rhine and Tub Boyle were the men he'd dealt with. Jubal had been an easy talker, with a scar on his jaw and pale-green eyes. Tub Boyle was built like a plow horse with almost no neck. He had a black moustache, but little hair on his head. Of the other two men, the buyer had only heard a single name for each: Deetz and Zig. Both wore cowboy garb and sombrero-type hats. No further description was necessary.

'Diamond A Ranch!' Travis declared. 'Those are Fulton Armstrong's men.'

Sparky gave an affirmative nod. 'They backed off and let us be, just so we would raise the cattle and do all the work. Then Armstrong gives the word and they take the cattle a day's ride from the railhead and leave us lying dead along the trail.' Sparky swore. 'At least we know where to find them.'

'We will need proof Armstrong ordered the attack,' Travis said.

Sparky had the buyer make out a deposition, writing down everything he had told them about the four men who sold him the cattle. When he had finished, Sparky put the paper inside his pocket.

'You think that paper will be enough?'

'Leave the proof to me, Capt'n. I'll take care of everything.'

From her perch in the rocks Rowena watched the

two distant riders. The men looked like the same pair who had accosted her in town. Her heart began to beat with some force and increased its tempo.

They're looking for me!

The realization struck her with a sudden terror. Her hideout was not visible from below, but her footpaths were quite worn from daily treks to the creek, along with the few trails she used to set and check on her traps and snares. If they discovered her tracks, the two men might leave their horses and begin to search the hills. If they located her den, she would be trapped outside, helpless and exposed to the elements with only the clothes on her back.

Rowena backed away from the ledge, careful not to dislodge any stones or to rise up enough to be silhouetted against the sky. She would keep watch and hope the two men moved on.

Sitting in the shade of a juniper, she felt the tickle of a breeze. Unlike the hotter days of summer, the movement of air hinted that cooler weather was not far off. It caused Rowena to worry again about the coming winter. Once the farmers had harvested the last of their gardens, she would have no food other than what she could find. The wild onions and berries were already gone and the currant bushes were picked clean. She knew of a few trees where she could collect some pine nuts, but it took a full day to make the trip up and back into the higher mountain range. Other than the occasional squaw-root (Buckeye told her it was also called yampa), and a little fruit from the yucca plants, there was nothing left to harvest for her winter supply of food.

The sound of voices carried up the side of the mountain. She eased forward again to get a peek. She saw that the two men were on different sides of the creek. They had found the place where the farm boys sometimes came to swim. That was a stroke of luck, as the presence of those tracks had them looking in the wrong direction. The words passed between the two men were not audible, but after a bit they continued down the creek.

Rowena let out a breath of relief. The two men had hunted along the stream's banks and not found any evidence of her being there. She desperately hoped they would not come back a second time.

Where else could she find shelter like the cave or secure an ally like Sue Dillard? Thinking of the storekeeper's wife, she recalled that she needed to add some corn and flour to her rations, but there was little to trade. There were few animals left in the hills. Farmers killed the smaller varmints that were a danger to their chickens and cowboys killed off other animals, such as coyotes, because they were a danger to their calves. Many of the locals also shot game for their own tables – rabbits, squirrels and quail or pine hens – so she had to compete for what little was left. As for the deer and elk, even if they weren't miles back in the hills, she had only a pistol and three shots. Not much chance she would bag a deer unless it walked up to her and committed suicide.

She could still fish the stream, but there were few fish and most were quite small. There was a muskrat or two, but she had no decent traps. Their teeth were sharp enough to cut through twine or wooden cages. The same was true for the beaver ponds high in the nearby mountains. Without proper traps for those critters, she would have few pelts to trade.

Rowena leaned back against a rock and closed her eyes. A great emptiness filled her chest, the hollow feeling of being alone, without anyone to confide in, without hope. Neville would continue his search until he found her. She knew that much about Walt's brother: he would not quit. In all of her travels she had not seen a single man wearing a badge. Every town was like Keylock. They couldn't afford to pay for a lawman, so someone like Mr Dillard handled the chore when it was needed. Well, she knew he could not handle men like Neville and Waco. If he stood up to them, they would kill him. Buckeye had told her many times that there was no law in this part of Colorado. He claimed a man had to keep his gun handy and deal with trouble on his own.

But I'm not a man!

Travis felt drained of strength. They had ridden solid for two days and he was not yet recovered from the bullet wound. The ache often penetrated deep into his chest and it would bleed some after moving around too much or riding a horse. After a few hours, he had to rest or ride doubled up to ease the pain.

His condition had not gone unnoticed by Sparky. 'Once we get back as far as Keylock, you can rest up a day or two while I go visit the US marshal and speak to a judge. I'll get warrants for the Diamond A crew and we'll have the law behind us.'

Travis grimaced inwardly at Sparky's decision. He didn't like the idea of waiting for a judge or marshal to act, but he was too weak to join in a fight just yet. He would do what Sparky suggested and hope his injury would heal.

After several hours of riding Travis brought up the plan again. He still didn't like being left behind and making Sparky do all the work.

'It's the best way to handle this,' his friend maintained. 'You about fell out of the saddle when we crossed that stream back there.'

'The horse stumbled.' Travis excused his reaction. 'It gave me a pretty good jolt.'

'That's what I mean, Capt'n. You need to take it easy for a few days. Can't expect to recover from a near mortal wound without proper rest.'

'I still ought to make the ride with you to Silver Crest and meet with the marshal. What if he doesn't believe you? What if you need someone to verify what we know to a judge?'

Sparky gave his head a shake. 'My word will do the trick. And it's forty miles of mountain trails betwixt Keylock and that mining town. You'd be lucky to stay in the saddle for five miles buck jumping up hill and over dale.'

'So I'm supposed to stay in town and wait for you?'

'Aye, Capt'n. Keylock is just up the road. I give it a look when we come through on our way to the railhead. There's a boarding house that you can hole up in while I make the trip to Silver Crest. The town isn't real big, but it does have a livery, freight office, saloon and store. It'll be a good place for you to rest up.'

'But that's three or four days wasted – you making the trip to Silver Crest and back to Keylock. If we don't act fast, Armstrong might either find out we're alive or spend the money.'

Sparky put on a stern look. 'You ain't going to be up to a fight until you heal some more. You take it easy for a couple days, while I take care of the legal aspect of this here chore. Don't worry, Capt'n, we'll get them polecats and figure a way to get our money back. But I'm telling you, this is the best way to handle things.'

Travis would have argued, but his head was throbbing with pain and his entire upper body felt on fire. He gave in without any more argument. 'All right, Sparky, but I'll wait for you at the junction to Silver Crest. I can set up camp next to the creek and get some rest there. Might try to catch a fish or two, but I'll take it easy and wait for you.'

'I'd feel better if you stayed at the boarding house.'

'No need to waste our money by paying for a room and having to board my horse at the livery. Plus, I'm used to sleeping on the trail. I'll throw up a lean-to before nightfall. There are plenty of trees and brush by the stream, so I won't have to work too hard.'

'I could help get you settled before I leave.'

'No, you need to get going. It's a long way to Silver Crest and back. We don't want to give the Diamond A any more time than we have to. If they get wind we survived, they will try and kill us both.'

'You're right on that count, Capt'n,' Sparky agreed. 'I'll be back as soon as I get the law on our side.'

When they reached the junction Travis watched his friend start up the rugged trail, leading the pack-animal behind. The terrain was rocky and uneven, rising over 1,000 feet between the junction at the main trail and the town of Silver Crest. He readily admitted he was not up to such a hard ride, not yet. He stripped the gear from his mare and put her on a tether where she could reach the creek and graze the grass along the bank. Rather than construct his shelter for the night, he spread out the saddle blanket and lay down to rest for a bit. His wound ached and he was drained of strength. A nap was what he needed. Once he'd gotten a couple hours' rest, he would try and catch a fish or two for his supper. There were a few clouds in the distance, but any storm would be late in the day, if it did decide to rain. He had plenty of time to round up wood for a fire and build a lean-to.

CHAPTER SEVEN

Neville's ears perked like a startled horse. 'An Indian you say?' he asked the farmer.

'That's what we've heard,' the man replied. 'Must be a pretty tame Redman, considering he trades for what he takes.'

'You're joshing me.'

'No,' the farmer stated, raising his hand as if he was about to swear on the Bible. 'He leaves behind berries or animal hides for whenever he takes from a garden. He even traded for some woman's bonnet.' His chest heaved with his hearty laugh. 'Can you imagine a wild Indian trying to pass himself off as a woman?'

Waco chuckled. 'That I'd like to see.'

But Neville wasn't laughing. 'And this is outside of the town of Keylock?'

'Yeah, that's west a fair piece . . . maybe fifty or

sixty miles. A salesman for farm tools was telling some of us about it the other day.'

'Guess we're safe here,' Waco said, grinning. 'Wouldn't want to get robbed by some Injun wearing a poke bonnet. That'd be downright humiliating.'

The farmer laughed again and then grew serious. 'Far as this woman you're looking for, I ain't heard nothing that would help you locate her.'

'She's a lot more dangerous than that Redman outside of Keylock, I can tell you that. She killed my brother and almost kilt me too.'

'Do tell?'

'Thanks for taking time to pass the day with us, friend.'

'Always got a minute to break up a day's work,' the farmer replied. 'Crops are in for the year, so there isn't near as much work waiting to be done.'

Neville and Waco gave him a wave and started down the trail. After a short way, Neville allowed himself a chortle. 'I do believe we've found our runaway.'

'Yeah,' Waco agreed. 'Stealing a poke bonnet and paying for what she takes. Squirrel don't want anyone hunting her down.'

'Too late for her to worry about that,' Neville sneered. 'We'll make Keylock by tomorrow or the next day. We can rest up a day or two and take a read on the lie of the land and the people around. We'll figure where the girl is at and make sure she don't have any friends or allies. Then we'll run her to ground.'

'We going to kill her when we find her?'

Neville's face twisted in a wicked smirk. 'Oh, yeah. Eventually.'

The air had become cooler at night and was slower to warm during the day, warning that the fall season was closing in. Rowena had done what she could to winterize her cavern home. A second blanket now covered the cave opening and she had rocks that would hold the corners in place, should there be a lot of wind. Conveniently, the cave faced the east and most winds blew from the southwest or north, saving her from the brunt of most storms.

Even with what she had gotten from Sue, her rations didn't last very long. The traps and snares were empty most days and the fishing was extremely poor. To stretch her supplies, she often made *skilly* for the morning meal – a little flour and water with a hint of salt, then fry it until it was a wafer-thin patty. However, it was not very tasty and did little to sate her hunger. At nights it was a couple pieces of jerky, from what little meat she had been able to store and whatever else she found during the day: usually, sunflower nuts and a few edible roots or seeds. She decided to visit some of the nearby farms the next few nights and forage for whatever crops remained. There might be a few remaining ears of corn or some potatoes, but she had nothing to offer in trade. She hated to resort to stealing food.

Setting aside her concerns, she decided to go down to the creek. She would fish for a bit and check her one muskrat snare. She doubted the trap was strong enough to hold the critter for long, but she might get lucky. She also took along the small dab of lotion she had extracted from the yucca root. It was the only shampoo she had used since Buckeye took her in. If it got warm enough, she would bathe and wash her hair.

Taking her short pole and line, she packed the rest of what she needed in her cloth bag. Then she made her way out of the den and took the trail down to the stream.

Tibbs dug his elbow into Ponch's ribs. His friend yelped from surprise and sat up abruptly.

'Yonder she comes,' Tibbs cackled like a hen who had just laid her first egg. 'See? I told you she had to be here!'

Ponch rose up to a sitting position so he could see the girl and nodded enthusiastically. 'Oh yeah, man! Just like you said. She sure enough has herself a rabbit hole back there in the hills.'

They watched her wind a snaky path, until she reached the water's edge. Then she disappeared among the high brush.

'Looks like she is gonna do some fishing,' Ponch commented.

Tibbs laughed. 'Bet she don't expect to catch us on her line, huh?'

'No siree,' Ponch agreed. 'How do you want to do this?'

'You go get the horses and then follow the creek until you catch up to me. I'll head her off, so she don't escape.'

Ponch groaned. 'What do we need the horses for?'

'We might want to leave in a hurry, once we've taken Miss High-and-Mighty down a step or two. Get going and I'll cut her off. We don't want to lose her.'

'All right, pard. I'm on my way.'

Tibbs moved at once, keeping his eyes on the portion of stream where he had last seen the girl. If she came downstream, he would have her quickly, as she would be coming right to him. If, however, she went upstream, he would have to hurry to keep her from getting too far away. If she was warned of his presence, the girl would take to cover like a frightened jackrabbit. No telling how long it would take to find her then.

Dodging boulders, loose shale rock, trees and

brush, Tibbs wound a hasty path, his excitement building. He kept a wary eye along the waterway, while trying not to make too much noise. If she was next to the water, the sound of it rushing past or going over rocks would help to hide his approach.

He had gone a hundred yards when he spied her. It was better than he hoped, as the girl was kneeling at the water's edge and had begun to wash her hair. Being preoccupied, she didn't see or hear him coming. He placed his feet carefully, weaving and slinking silently forward.

Abruptly, as if the girl had a sixth sense, she stopped working some soapy stuff in her hair and looked around. Tibbs quickly hunkered down behind the weeds and brush. The feral female blinked against the water in her eyes, listening.

Like trying to sneak up on a spooked chipmunk, he mused. *The only thing missing is a tail twitching nervously.*

Endless seconds passed.

Tibbs remained squatted down and waited, fascinated by the girl's canny vigilance. She hadn't moved so much as a hair, even though water and suds slid down the side of her neck and soaked the collar of her dress. It was the same outfit she had worn in town, buckskin skirt and faded yellow blouse. Her jacket, fishing pole and a cloth bag were within her arm's reach. This was a very careful woman.

Eventually, thinking she was safe, the white savage rotated back to the creek and ducked low, plunging her hair into the water. One quick rinse and she hurriedly grabbed up a ragged towel to dry off.

Tibbs didn't wait any longer. In the blink of an eye, she could snatch up her things and bolt for the underbrush. He rose up and raced across the open ground. The girl sensed his approach – too late!

By the time she got her feet under her, he hit her with a flying tackle and dragged her to the ground. They rolled over together and he used his size advantage to get the better of her. That was when he felt several strips of fire ignited along his left cheek. She'd raked him a good one!

'Damn your hide!' Tibbs wailed. 'I'll knock the stuffing out of you!'

The wildcat screamed – more a screech of rage and frustration at being caught than from fear; loud enough to cause a ringing in his ears.

Wrapping his arms around a full-grown tiger would have been about the same as trying to pin the wild woman to the ground. She wasn't very big, but she was wiry, determined and vicious. She bit, kicked and clawed at his arms and face, twisting and battling with all of her strength.

Tibbs finally restrained her physically, clamping a hand on each of her wrists and using his knees to pin her legs. It wasn't quite enough. She bucked under his weight and when he leaned forward to force her down, she reared up and butted her forehead against his mouth, rattling his teeth and splitting his lip.

'Ye-ow!' he yelped. Growing more furious at her resistance, he bodily slammed her against the ground – once, twice and a third time. The harsh punishment knocked the wind out of her and she lay dazed. 'I've had it with you, you ornery, feisty she-cat!' Tibbs snarled. 'You settle down or I'll—'

But she had only ceased her struggle long enough to catch her breath. She swung a leg up and actually kicked him on the side of the head! Tibbs was nearly unseated by her remarkably agile feat. Enraged now, he hauled off and punched her squarely in the jaw.

The blow subdued her momentarily, allowing him time to place a knee on both of her forearms to pin them down, while planting his weight in the middle of her chest. He was through wrestling and allowing her to fight. Satisfied he had her completely restrained, he began to tear at her blouse.

'Now I'll show you who's the boss, woman!' he ranted. 'I'm going to—'

Abruptly, something grabbed hold of the back of his collar and he was jerked upward and off of the girl. Before his brain had a chance to realize what was happening, he was spun about. A set of rock-hard knuckles appeared fleetingly before his eyes, then exploded against the bridge of his nose!

Travis had been half-asleep, with his fishing line in the water, when he heard the desperate cry of a woman. As he was only a short way upstream, he had hurried toward the sound. He arrived in time to see a scruffy-looking man subdue and strike a woman. When the man began to rip at her clothing, he raced forward and stopped him.

The attacker was blinded by the punch between his eyes. He waved his arms about and tried to get his bearings, but Travis hit him a second time, squashing his nose and knocking him flat on his back. It was fortunate that Travis had the advantage of surprise, because his wound complained bitterly about engaging in fisticuffs. That second blow had caused a scorching jolt all through his upper body. However, the two wallops were enough to stun the varmint. Travis pulled his gun and moved back a few steps to cover him.

Suddenly, he heard horses, moving fast.

'Look out!' the girl cried a warning – about one split second late!

The rider bore down on him with another horse in tow. Travis spun about, trying to get out of the way, but the man kicked out with his boot and hit Travis solidly in the chest. An explosion of pain detonated throughout his upper torso as he was propelled backwards into a thicket of bitterbrush. Both paralyzed from the immense agony and tangled in the shrub, he managed to cling to his gun.

'Get on!' he heard a man yell. Travis knew that both men were escaping on their horses. Fighting against the blackness, he feebly waved the gun, as if he was trying to take aim. It took the remainder of his consciousness to manage the feat, but he was rewarded by the sound of the two men's hasty retreat. Feeling the girl was safe, he let go of all awareness.

CHAPTER EIGHT

Within the tranquil world of darkness, something stung his cheek. A few moments passed and it happed again. This time, Travis managed to get his eyes open. He discovered he had been pulled from the brush and a woman with wet, tangled hair and a torn blouse, hovered over him with a curious expression on her face.

'Come on, mister, wake up!' she urged him. Then with a sarcastic disdain, 'You ain't much for toughness, are you?'

He tried to speak, but no words were at hand.

The girl remained adamant. 'We've got to get out of here before those two come back.'

Travis made an effort to sit up, but a spasm of pain flattened him back on the ground. He grimaced and put a hand to his chest. Inside his jacket was a dampness he recognized; his wound was bleeding again.

The girl immediately showed alarm and her eyes grew wide. 'Flying buffalo chips!' she exclaimed. 'I didn't know they shot you!'

'No,' he gasped, 'it's from an old wound. It had about healed.'

She helped him to sit up and pulled back his shirt to see the rusty stain on the cloth bandage. It had bled quite a bit, but seemed to have stopped.

'How's the back?' he asked.

Her brows lifted. 'The back of what?'

He reached over with his right arm and shrugged his jacket down over his shoulder. 'The other side of the wound,' he informed the girl.

She pulled his shirt until she could peek at the spot. 'Looks fine to me. No blood on this side.'

'That's good.' He tried to keep his mind working. 'You find my hat?'

'Yes, it's on your head.' Travis glanced up to see the brim, he gave a slight bob of his head and said, 'Oh.' The girl added, 'I never seen one with such a fancy hatband. Is it real silver?'

'I bought it off a gambler who had lost his last dime. He said it hadn't brought him any luck, but it might bring me some.'

'You believe in stuff like that – a lucky hat?'

Instead of answering, he advised her, 'My horse is a short way upstream. I set up camp next to the creek.'

'I'll get your horse,' she told him. 'You best sit here and try not to bleed.'

'Yes, ma'am, sounds like good advice.'

The girl started to leave his side but hesitated. 'I'm beholden to you for butting in like you did.'

'Never figured rescuing a damsel in distress was butting in.'

A slight smile tugged at the corners of her mouth. 'Oh, that's what you were doing, rescuing a damsel, huh?'

'Didn't do such a great job of it, did I?'

'You done fine,' she countered. 'Those two lowlife cowpokes didn't know you were wounded. They scampered out of here like their shirt tails was on fire.'

'Lucky for both of us that they didn't have the grit for a fight.'

'I'll be back with your horse.'

'It looks like rain,' Travis said. 'I put up a lean-to where I spent last night.'

'I've got better shelter for a storm,' she answered back. Then she was gone, moving like a ghost through the brush. Her feet were swift and she didn't seem to make a sound.

So, Travis Clay, what kind of strange creature have you got yourself mixed up with?

Rowena struck down the lean-to and located the

stranger's horse. The animal spooked a little at her approach, but she spoke softly to it and was able to get her saddled. She tied the man's belongings behind the saddle and led the horse back along the creek.

Her rescuer was unconscious again, but he came awake enough that she was able to get him on his horse. She hitched his belt over the saddle horn to help him stay seated, and told him to hold on with both hands. Then she started off along the path to her secluded abode. It was slow going, having to be careful so the man didn't fall off.

Once she was as close to the cave entrance as she could get, the real chore began. Her rescuer was groggy from his pain. When she pulled him from the saddle, he fell right on top of her!

Rowena would have panicked if the man had been conscious, but he was basically a great weight she had to maneuver. She coaxed him up to his feet and ducked under his arm so it was around her shoulders. As the clouds opened and a downpour of rain began, she used her strong legs to support much of the man's weight and they made a slow ascent to the cave.

When Rowena eventually had the man lying down she took a few moments to recoup her strength. The workout had left her weakened, but she knew she had to complete the chores necessary before she could rest.

After tethering the horse and stripping off the saddle she brought most of the man's belongings to the cave. The saddle was too heavy for her so she left it under some brush. Then she turned to the task of building up her fire and making the man comfortable. He had exhausted what strength he had and appeared to be sleeping soundly.

As was her habit, when upset, frightened or filled with anxiety, she hunkered down and began to rock back and forth. Instead of humming a familiar tune, she studied the newcomer and wondered what kind of man he was. He was not overly handsome, but he had pleasant features and looked capable. He had a firm jaw, brown hair and eyes, and had spoken to her in an easy manner, as if rescuing a person was something he did matter-of-factly.

One other thing stood out. He was clean-shaven and had neatly shorn hair. Buckeye, Walt and Tibbs, most of the other men she had been around or seen in her travels or at the trading post, had facial hair. Some kept trimmed moustaches while others wore beards. She had seldom seen a grown man who didn't have a host of whiskers. She stopped rocking, hesitated, then reached over and gently touched the man's cheek. It was as if he were a dandy, one who presented himself as a proper gentleman.

She smiled, thinking of what Buckeye would say if he could see her now. *Strange looking critter you've brought home, Squirrel, but I reckon you can keep him if you want!*

Tibbs pulled his poncho over his head, cursing the sudden downpour of rain. Once his hat was back on, he gingerly wiped the water from his face and ran his tongue over his split lip. The swelling around the bridge of his nose had spread to the flesh about his eyes and they were both puffy. Adding to his misery, the deep nail scratches stung from exposure to moisture. The wildcat woman had been saved by some meddling stranger who had busted his nose. He cursed vehemently and lamented about his woeful condition to Ponch.

His partner was sympathetic. 'Yep, you're gonna have twin shiners, and that's the truth. Remember Long-handle Jones, the way both his eyes went black after that barkeep busted him in the snoot? I swear you'll be a looking like him for a couple weeks at least.'

Tibbs grumbled another curse and paused to spit. The taste of blood was still in his mouth from the girl's head-butt. 'Should have stuck around and kilt that nosy jasper.'

'I dunno, Tibbs. He pulled that smoke wagon like he knew which end to point. We was lucky he fell into that brush and got tangled up long enough for us to get out of there. Don't know how we'd have done in a shoot-out.'

'You're probably right, Ponch,' Tibbs allowed. 'I couldn't see much of anything after he attacked me from behind. It was all I could do to get on my horse.'

'Besides that, the little wildcat began tossing rocks. Hit me a couple good ones before we got away.'

'Yeah, she nailed me in the middle of the back with one too. We'll both be sporting bruises from her rock throwing.'

'We'll shore 'nuff pay them back,' Ponch vowed. 'We'll find a way.'

'Yes, soon as I get healed up, we'll track them down and make them damn sorry they ever crossed our paths.'

'Where do you think that guy came from?' Ponch queried aloud. 'We didn't see any riders before the gal showed up.'

'I don't know. We were watching downriver all morning. He must have come in from the junction to Silver Crest.'

'Round the bend,' Ponch agreed. 'That sounds about right. We couldn't have seen him coming.'

Tibbs spat again, irate that he couldn't breathe though his nose. The blood had stopped, but the airways were completely blocked. Every step of the horse caused his entire face to throb and the blasted rain only made things worse. He would go see Sally-Mae at the saloon. She not only ran the bar and served drinks, she was a midwife and about the only one who knew any doctoring for miles around. She had straightened Jones's nose so it didn't look half bad. Of course, Jones had been ugly as sin his whole life, so it was hard to tell any difference. Still, he would have Sally-Mae do what she could and take it easy for a day or two.

Soon as the swelling was gone, they would go find that wild woman and her pal again. This time, the interfering mongrel wouldn't catch him looking the other way. He and Ponch would beat him to within an inch of death . . . then finish the job!

Travis's brain fired sporadically, like distant lightning flashes against a dark sky. There were bits of illumination, visions, images, and a smattering of lucid moments. The rest was black, ominous and lost within a thick, nebulous haze. He had a memory of getting on his horse – though he'd had considerable help – then being jostled and pounded unmercifully by the horse's hard climb up an endless mountain. When he eventually felt himself being dragged to the ground, it was another maze of emotions and dreams, as if he was less than conscious, yet forced to obey commands to walk, climb and even crawl.

He vaguely remembered getting wet from the rain, but the chill had long since gone. His dreamless sleep lasted for what seemed only a few minutes before he was being shaken awake.

'Mister, you need to eat something,' came a muffled voice.

He decided there was no reason to wake up just to eat. Sleeping seemed the better idea.

'Mister!' The voice was amplified tenfold. 'You open your eyes or I'll shove a fistful of beans down your throat and you can choke on them!'

Travis rousted himself to consciousness and groaned. 'Can't say much for your bedside manner, ma'am.'

He heard a slight gasp and realized the girl must have been concerned that he had slipped into a coma. He'd seen a man do that one time; slept until he died for lack of food and water. There might be worse ways to die, but he wasn't ready to be planted under six feet of dirt.

Opening his eyes, he discovered a flickering light from a nearby fire and spied the face of a child. His brain function began to work and he realized it was not a child, but a young woman with youthful and rather innocent features. Her hazel eyes glistened in the glow of the flames and he noticed that she

102

had petite features and a slight overbite that gave her lips a rather sensuous arc. Slender of figure, but she was definitely not a child. He recalled the scream, the fight, and her talking to him, but this was the first time he had really looked at her.

'I heated some beans from your saddle-bags,' she began. 'I . . . I also prepared . . .' she was so halting in her speech that Travis frowned up at her. 'I took a few of your dried apple pieces,' she admitted, a crimson color spreading across her cheeks. 'I didn't eat too many,' she hurried to add. 'But, well, I haven't had any apples for a long time.'

'I don't mind,' he reassured her. 'You're welcome to share whatever food I have.'

She looked surprised that he was not the slightest bit upset. 'But they belong to you and I don't have anything to trade.'

Travis took a quick inventory of his surroundings. It was a cavern of maybe fifteen feet across at the widest point and about twenty feet deep. He saw the fireplace, complete with a rock foundation for cooking. Near by was a neatly folded dress, a couple pieces of cloth, a jacket and a few sewing trinkets. There was no table, but he took note of a small collection of cooking utensils and a water jug. He was lying on a buckskin mat and had been covered with a single army-style blanket.

'Nice place you have here,' he remarked. 'Don't

get a lot of visitors, I would guess.'

'Only the occasional varmint or insect,' she replied.

'How long have I been out?'

'It's after dark. I didn't want you sleeping all night without something to eat. Having bled some, I figured you'd need some vittles to gain back your strength.'

Travis used his good arm to push himself gingerly up to a sitting position. The small fire caused shadows to dance on the cave walls, but it was warm and dry. A blanket covered the opening, which looked to be about four-foot square and a crack in the rock ceiling made a natural chimney, so the smoke from the fire filtered to the outside.

'So this is your home.' It was a statement. 'Looks like the kind of place a bear would choose come time for hibernation.'

'Only seen one bear since I've been here and he skedaddled quick enough.'

Travis observed the pan of beans sitting next to the fire. 'You eat yet?'

'Like I said, I took a few slices of dried apple.'

'Well, one can of beans won't hold us both. Put in the other one too.'

She displayed a worried look. 'But that's all you have, other than for a little more dried fruit and a couple strips of jerky.'

'I was going to ride to town and buy a few things

104

tomorrow. I'm waiting for a friend of mine. He won't be back for another day or two.'

She didn't argue, using a knife to open the can. She dumped the beans into the pan and set it over the fire to warm.

'What are you doing out here by yourself?' he asked.

The girl kept her back to him, stirring the beans with a spoon so they wouldn't burn. He knew she had heard him but gave no indication she would answer.

'Sorry,' he apologized. 'I guess that's really none of my business. It's just that you're the first female hermit I ever come across.'

'What's your name?' she asked, without commenting on his remarks.

'Travis Clay, Miss. I work on a ranch about a hundred miles from here. Some cowhands and me were taking a herd of cattle to the railhead when we were ambushed. The bushwhackers killed two of my friends and I was left for dead. Would have died too, except Sparky, a fellow who has been with me since I joined the army, was off getting supplies for us. He tended to me until I could ride. We know who stole the cattle, so he rode up to Silver Crest to visit the US marshal and get warrants for the rustlers. I was camped by the stream to rest up and wait for him to return.'

She had the beans warm and tried to hand him the pan and spoon.

'You first, ma'am,' he said. 'My folks didn't raise me to be a ruffian without manners.'

The girl hesitated only a moment. When she began to eat, he could see she was practically starving. She didn't wolf down her food like an animal, but her expression showed she was savoring the flavor of each bite. After only eating a small amount, she offered the pan to him once more.

'That's way too much for me,' he said, raising a hand to stop from taking the pan. 'You'll have to make more of a dent than that.'

Her eyes narrowed, suspicious, yet not completely certain as to whether he was being polite or truthful. Regardless, she took a few more bites, eating a full one-half of the portion, before offering the beans to him again.

Travis ate what was left, then watched the girl carefully clean and put away the single spoon and pan. It looked as if several different-sized pans, a hunting knife and the one old spoon were about all the she had.

'I told you my name and how I came to be here. I think that should at least earn me your name.'

She gazed at him for a long moment. The look was one of evaluation, as if she was trying to determine his character, honesty and trustworthiness all in one all-inclusive scrutiny.

'My name is Rowena Jansen,' she began. Then, without further coaxing, she told him her life's story, ending with Buckeye being murdered. The culmination of her story was the fear that Neville Pockman might have told the law she had killed both his brother and Buckeye, then stole his horse.

'I did take Neville's horse,' she admitted, 'and I grabbed what little money me and Buckeye had saved, but it was because I knew Neville would kill me. He won't stop looking for me until he finds me.'

'What about the two men earlier today?'

'Those jackals have a place down the road a few miles. Their names are Tibbs and Ponch. They think they can do whatever they want to me, 'cause I'm hiding out like an outlaw. I'm guessing they know I can't go to the law.' She harrumphed. 'Not that there is any real law around here anyway.'

'Tomorrow morning we'll get some supplies. Where did you put my horse?'

'In a cove, just below us. It's a safe place and there's plenty of grass for the night.'

'All right. We'll go to town and pick up enough to get us by until Sparky – he's the friend I mentioned – gets back.'

'What do you mean: *get us by*?' she wanted to know. 'I never volunteered to have you move in for several days.'

'I'm not going to leave you unprotected. Those two coyotes know you are in these hills. If they come back looking for you, I'll make them durned sorry when they find us.'

She displayed the hint of a grin. 'You sound just like Buckeye when you talk that way.'

'Oh, yeah?'

'He had to tame his language once he took me in. He told me he was a cussin' fool before I come along. Once I was staying with him, instead of using bad words, he said things like *durn* or *dag nab-it*.'

'And maybe *flying buffalo chips*?'

She laughed. 'I didn't know you'd even heard me. You kind of looked like a rabbit I once clobbered in the head with a rock – dazed and running in circles.'

He enjoyed the way her eyes lit up when she laughed. 'Anyway,' he said, getting back to their current situation, 'I'll keep an eye out for those two, whether you let me stay in the cave or I do it from outside.'

'What makes you so sure you can protect me?'

'I fought in the war and I'm a better than average shot with either a pistol or rifle. If those two show their faces around here, I'll pepper their hides and send them running for cover.'

'Buckeye said most men who brag are the kind who talk big but can't back up their words.'

'He did, huh? What else did Buckeye teach you?'

'That real men don't cry.'

'I agree with that. A man shouldn't break down and sob in public. I suppose a few tears are allowed if you've lost someone you loved, or maybe your favorite horse or dog.'

'He also said real men put their women folk and children first, and that a man's worth ain't figured by how much money he has, but what good he does.'

'Sounds like Buckeye had some wisdom.'

'I seen him for his faults too, but he treated me good. He took care of me and I took care of him.'

'Well, then, that's what I'm going to do too.' At the curious wrinkling of her brow, he said, 'You've taken care of me, so I aim to take care of you.' Before she could argue, he finished, 'Until Sparky returns. Then you can decide what you want to do.'

'I told you, I can't—'

'When we go into town I'll send off a telegram and see if there is any kind of warrant out for you. If not, then you can find a job working at a hotel, laundry or restaurant, something where you can earn a living. You can't spend the winter up here; you'll starve or freeze, or both.'

'And if there is a warrant of some kind?'

He grinned, 'Depends on the amount of the reward.'

'Oh, that's going to make me sleep better,' she quipped.

'Let's see what tomorrow brings. Maybe you've been running for nothing.'

'Neville won't stop looking, whether I'm wanted by the law or not. I seen Walt kill Buckeye, but that don't matter to him. I killed his brother and he won't be happy until he kills me.'

'How about we worry about one thing at a time?'

The nearly smokeless fire had died out. Rowena removed a few hot coals and placed them inside a coffee pot, then she said, 'You get some rest. I've got your saddle blanket and a warm jacket.'

'There's room for both of us under this blanket,' he offered. 'We're both fully dressed and I'm in no condition to have any amorous notions.'

She laughed. 'I never heard a man use that word *amorous* before.'

He again enjoyed the sound of her mirth. When thinking of his past, he had never faced the kind of challenges she'd had. Rowena had truly had a hard life. Much as he wanted to catch the four killers he and Sparky were after, he also wanted to help this young woman. Lying in the dark, he wondered how he could do both.

CHAPTER NINE

Travis was awake when Rowena got up from where she had spent the night, huddled in a blanket like an Indian squaw. She moved over to the cave entrance and pulled the improvised curtain aside a few inches. It was first light and, for a few moments, she remained perched at the opening, staring out to study the surroundings.

'Oh, buffalo chips!' she muttered. 'You would show up today.'

Travis frowned at her odd expression and did a hasty, one-handed, down-on-his-knees, crawl over to her side. 'Someone coming?'

Rowena scowled. 'That sneaky, good-for-nothing, sage hen is back.' She extended her arm and pointed. 'She's been teasing me for about a month. Soon as I move the blanket enough to get out of the cave she flies off, and I don't get another look at her until a day or two later.'

Travis had to look hard. The rain had dampened the earth, but not enough to make it muddy, and the brush and grass had only a slight glistening from the remaining moisture. He searched until he eventually spotted the top of the bird's head. 'You could try a shot from here.'

'That's near impossible from this distance. Besides, I've only got three bullets left. If she ever showed when I was outside, I could knock her down with a rock. I'm pretty good at throwing rocks.'

The girl didn't notice Travis pull his gun. He waited until the bird lifted its head above the sagebrush and fired!

Rowena squealed in surprise, threw her hands to her ears and lamented, 'Flying buffalo chips! What're you doing?'

'Shooting the bird for you.'

She moved the blanket aside again and looked out. 'You couldn't have hit her from here. It must be twenty steps away and there was nothing showing but her head.'

'Might want to check anyway,' he told her.

Rowena went out of the cave, scampering around and through the brush. When she reached the spot, she squealed in delight like a child who had found a hidden piece of candy.

'You got 'um!' she declared, lifting the bird up by

the feet. 'Oh, she's a fine fat one too.'

He smiled at her jubilation as she made her way back to the cave. She reached inside the door and removed an old flour sack. 'I save most of the feathers,' she explained, beginning to pluck the sage hen. 'I still can't believe it. You shot the critter's head right off.'

'Well, most people don't eat anything above the neck anyway.'

She paused from her chore and regarded him with a look of wonderment. 'Buckeye could hit a buffalo from a quarter mile off, but he couldn't have hit that bird, not having a target no bigger than a hen's egg.'

'I told you I was a better shot than most with a gun.'

'Yes, and I'm sorry I accused you of bragging. It sure ain't bragging when you can do what you say.'

'Finish up with the bird and we'll go into town. We can pick up some fixings to go with the hen for our supper.'

'You seem determined to stay here with me,' she said.

'Only if you sleep on your own bed tonight. I've got a saddle and blankets that do me nicely.'

She continued to pluck the feathers, then took her knife and dressed out the bird in about two minutes flat. Once she had the bird tucked away in a cool spot, she uttered an '*ahem,*' and gave him a meaningful look. He realized she needed a few minutes alone and rose slowly to his feet, although he had to duck down, as the cave roof was less than six feet high in many places.

Travis picked up his saddle blanket and hoped his saddle hadn't gotten too wet, sitting out all night. 'I'll walk down and saddle my mare. You get ready and I'll meet you at the bottom of the hill. OK?'

'I'll be there in five minutes.'

Travis moved slowly, so as to not jar his wound. The injury hadn't bled during the night, so he figured it was on the mend again. He had to be careful and not do anything to jeopardize his recovery. It was no easy task, but he managed to saddle his horse using only one arm. The hardest part was when he had to tighten the chinch. Next, he led the mare over some of the worst ground, so as not to risk any sudden jolts. By the time he reached the bottom of the hill, the girl was moving down the hill to join him.

Rowena did not miss Travis's appreciative inspection upon her arrival at their meeting place. She had donned the brown dress, which fit properly after many hours of hemming and numerous adjustments. She had also brushed her hair and pulled it back, using a slender thread of rawhide.

114

He mounted first, but used his good right arm to help pull her up behind him. They rode to town together, mostly in a comfortable silence. That much seemed odd to Rowena, for she had never been alone with any man for any length of time, other than Buckeye. The security of his company was also reassuring, as Travis seemed an honorable man and a gentleman. Funny, but her only impression of a gentleman had been her father, and that was from back when she was only twelve years old.

'I'll drop you at the store, while I go over to the stage and freight office. I saw a sign on the door that read it is also the telegraph office.'

'What supplies should I get?'

'Anything we'll need for the next coupla days.' He turned his head to look back at her. 'I shouldn't be but a few minutes.'

'How long until you get an answer back from the marshal?'

'If he's in his office and gets the message right away, maybe by the time we leave. Otherwise, it will probably be tomorrow.'

'I don't feel right, you spending your money on me.'

'If I took a room and ate at the local eatery, I'd spend a whole lot more.'

'Buckeye never taught me much about proper folks,' she said. 'But I know there are some social-

115

type rules against a man and a woman sharing the same room. I can tell you're a trustworthy sort, but I'm not sure it's right or proper for you to be staying with me.'

'You're the one who took me in,' he reminded her.

'Yes, but you got hurt defending me. I owed you.'

'I can always set up my camp outside somewhere. I don't want you feeling uncomfortable about our arrangement.'

'No,' she said a bit too quickly. 'I was only saying what some might think.'

'Well, I won't tell anyone if you don't.'

'How about the supplies? Mrs Dillard knows I don't have any money.'

'You can introduce me as a distant relative ... maybe a cousin. That ought to protect your reputation.'

'A cousin from when and where?'

Travis sighed. 'When you set to make up a story, you want a lot of background to go with it, don't you?'

'All right, you're a cousin who used to hunt buffalo with Buckeye. That ought to do.'

'Except I've never taken a shot at a buffalo. I wouldn't know what to do with one after I killed it.'

'I know all about that part of the chore,' she assured him. 'Me and Buckeye made our living hunting buffalo for several years. I must have skinned a couple hundred of them critters.'

'You've had an adventurous life. Whatever story you tell, I'll back you up.'

'It's only got to sound good if Mrs Dillard asks. I'm hoping she won't, 'cause I don't lie worth beans.'

'Shouldn't have to do much explaining. We only need to buy a few things at the store.'

She didn't continue the conversation further as they were entering town. Travis stopped at the front of the store and she slid to the ground.

'If those two mangy curs from yesterday show up, you come get me straight away,' he warned her.

'I'll be fine,' she said. Then she watched him ride the short way to the stage office and carefully dismount. He still moved about as stiff as if he was made of wood, but he tied off his horse at the hitching post and went inside.

Mrs Dillard was adding a few eggs to a basket on the counter as Rowena entered. She glanced up to greet a potential customer and a wide smile lit up her face.

'Rowena!' she said happily. 'Land sakes! That dress fits you beautifully. You did a wonderful job of taking it in.'

A flush of pleasure warmed Rowena's cheeks. 'It is very nice material, and I really wanted to thank you again. It's the nicest dress I ever owned.'

'Is everything all right?' Mrs Dillard asked, being motherly. 'I've been worried about you, living out there all alone.'

'It's not so bad. But there isn't a lot of game in the lower hills any more, so I don't have as much to trade.'

'You are about as thin as a stalk of straw, dear. I really think you should let me and Barney help you.'

'That's very kind of you, but I'm doing real good. In fact, I've come to buy a few things today.'

The woman's smile faded, replaced by a serious expression. 'I seen that no good Tibbs yesterday – one of those two rowdies who gave you grief when you were here last time. Looked as if he'd been kicked in the face by a mule.' When Rowena offered nothing, she continued. 'I suspect someone gave that worthless skunk his come-upping.'

'He's not in town today, is he?'

'I don't think so. He visited Sally-Mae, over at the saloon – she does a little doctoring. Then he and his pal rode out. Can't say he looked any better when he left.' She smirked, 'Then again, he wasn't nothing special to start with.'

Rowena almost blurted out what had happened, but she didn't want Sue's husband, as the acting lawman, getting involved. He might get hurt and she would hate for that to happen. She set the notion aside and began to figure a menu for three days.

'Funny you should be sending this wire,' the old gent said, beginning to tap on his telegraph key.

Travis waited, but he didn't offer any more until he prodded him with, 'Why is that?'

A reply tapping came down the line. 'We're through to Silver Crest,' he informed Travis. Then, as he again began sending the message, he looked up at him. 'Another man was asking the marshal's office about the same thing, not more'n some time back. He seemed real concerned if there was a warrant out for anyone connected with the death of a man called Buckeye Summerville, or if they'd been contacted by a woman named Rowena.'

'I happen to know who killed Buckeye,' Travis replied. 'It was two brothers, Walt and Neville Pockman.'

The telegrapher snorted. 'Figures.'

Travis again wondered what that meant, but the old boy was not forthcoming without being coaxed. 'Was it Neville Pockman who sent off the wire?'

'Telegrams are confidential.' He cocked a bushy eyebrow. 'Part of my job is to keep my mouth shut.'

'What about any warrants on Rowena Janson?'

'Didn't get anything on a gal by that name what-soever.'

'How about the information you got back about Buckeye? That would pretty much answer my other question one way or the other.'

'I've already sent your wire, sonny. You saying you don't want to wait around for the answer?'

'Not if you know what the answer will be.'

The telegrapher grinned. 'You've already paid me for sending it. Running you down to give you the reply don't pay a cent.' Travis nodded his agreement. 'So I'll tell you that the marshal's office don't know anything about anyone named Buckeye Summerville . . . not if he's dead or alive or ever lived at all. As for the Rowena lady, there was nothing on her either. However, that Pockman character asked if I'd seen anyone to fit her description.'

Travis understood. Rowena had been fearful that Neville would try to pin a murder on her, either the old boy's or Walt's. It made sense. There was only her word that Walt had killed Buckeye and no proof she hadn't killed Walt in cold blood.

Travis placed a silver dollar on the counter for the telegrapher. 'Should that fellow Pockman happen by again, I'd as soon he didn't know I was checking on this. I wouldn't want him putting a bullet in my back for being curious.'

The man stuck the coin into his pocket. 'Don't rightly remember why I sent this here wire to the marshal's office just now. Reckon I won't bother writing down the answer.'

Travis thanked him and left the office. When he reached the store he saw that Rowena had gathered a handful of supplies. He would have bet his horse that she had planned out exactly how much she needed for the meals . . . with not a scrap left over.

'Add a pound of coffee, a couple pounds of flour, six more eggs, a couple tins of milk and a wedge of cured bacon,' he said to the woman at the counter. 'Also a dozen candy sticks and some salt and sugar too.'

Rowena frowned at him. 'I can't get all that in my bag.'

'I've got an empty flour sack,' the woman offered, hurrying to gather the things Travis had added.

Shortly, Travis was paying for the goods. Rowena stood by awkwardly until he took the sack. Then she smiled timorously at the woman clerk.

'This is Mr Clay, my cousin, Mrs Dillard,' she stated simply.

Holding the sack in his good hand, Travis couldn't lift his left arm enough to tip his hat, so he tipped his head in acknowledgment. 'Pleasure to meet you, ma'am.'

Sue returned the smile. 'You take good care of her, Mr Clay. She seems a very special young lady.'

'Yes, ma'am, I couldn't agree with you more.'

He pushed open the door and held it long enough for Rowena to exit the store. This time, he let her get on the horse first, so he could pass up the sack of groceries. Then he used his good right arm and mounted by swinging his leg over the horse's neck. As soon as they were moving he cocked his head enough to speak over his shoulder to Rowena.

'You're safe enough from the law, but you were right about Pockman. He and another fella came through here looking for you.'

He heard her suck in her breath at the news. 'What about Buckeye's death?'

'It doesn't appear that anyone reported it, unless it was to say he'd died from natural causes.'

'Yes,' she said bitterly, 'It's *natural* to die when you can't get any air to your lungs.'

'Sounds as if Pockman was concerned you might have talked to the law.'

'I thought about it, but I never saw a real lawman during all the time I was running. Mr Dillard does some lawman stuff here in Keylock, but he's just the owner of the general store. He doesn't even carry a gun.'

'Won't be any proof of how Buckeye died. Being smothered with a pillow, it would look the same as if his heart gave out. And I imagine Pockman buried him to cover their tracks.'

'Then it would be my word against Neville's,' she concluded.

'And Walt is dead, so he has paid for his crime.'

Rowena changed the subject. 'Why did you buy so much extra stuff?'

'Those two men who attacked you know where to find you,' he said. 'I'm not going to leave you to fend for yourself.'

'I'm good at fending for myself,' she replied. 'I was doing all of the work for Buckeye and me the past couple years.'

'Pockman is bound to come back looking for you,' he warned.

'What do you think I should do?'

'You can't go through a Colorado winter living in a cave,' he stated. 'You need to find a place where you can work and be safe, with a roof over your head.'

'Mrs Dillard would help, if I stayed near Keylock.'

'Even if Pockman didn't find you, there's still those two jaspers from yesterday to deal with.'

'So what am I supposed to do, Mr Clay?'

'I'm just saying, you can't stay around Keylock.'

Rowena fell silent for a short time, before she eventually asked the question. 'Where am I supposed to go?'

'With me and Sparky,' Travis replied. 'We'll find you a safe place.'

'You're chasing the murderers who killed your friends and stole your herd of cattle. You don't have time to be looking for a home for me.'

Travis continued the ride, without giving a reply. Indeed, he had no idea what to do with the girl, but he wasn't going to leave her to deal with so much trouble on her own. Once they reached the rocky trail beyond the junction to Silver Crest, he slowed the mare and tucked his left arm tightly against his chest. Every stumble and jump by the horse raked his wounded side, but he made it to the cove without doubling over or falling from the back of his horse.

Once the animal was watered from a drainage-ditch pool and picketed for the day, he and Rowena made their way up to her dwelling. It was slow going, with her carrying the groceries and him lugging his saddle and rifle.

When they reached the cave, he sagged down to rest, while Rowena set about preparing a small feast. She roasted the game hen and made some sweet bread. All the while, she never said another word about his proposal.

CHAPTER TEN

'How'd you know where to find me, Spartan?' the US marshal asked.

'I wired your office once we tracked the stolen cattle to the railhead. They said you were up here looking into some trouble.'

'Battle over some mining rights,' the marshal replied. 'What do you need?'

Sparky showed the written deposition to Konrad Ellington. 'You see the buyer signed his name at the bottom,' he said. 'Promised to testify if we needed him to.'

'I'll bet he did,' Konrad replied. 'Better than admitting he knew he was buying stolen cattle.'

'I might have mentioned that when I got his promise.'

Konrad looked up with interest. 'Spartan, you were a solid deputy the couple times I needed you.

I've no doubt you're telling me the truth about all this. But how do you know this Armstrong character is guilty of anything?'

'He was trying to run the Nalens out of the country before me and Travis Clay came back from the war. The Capt'n, as I call him, drew a line in the sand and Armstrong never crossed it.'

'Sounds like a good man.'

'Best I ever knew ... 'cept maybe for you, Marshal.'

Konrad smiled. 'I'll have the judge issue warrants for the four men you know are involved. As for Armstrong, you'll need one of those men to turn on him to have proof of his involvement.'

'I understand,' Sparky replied.

'You did say Travis Clay?'

Sparky wrinkled his brow. 'Yeah, that's the Capt'n.'

'My office answered a query from him earlier today.' Sparky did not hide his shock, while Konrad continued. 'He was asking if there was news about the death of a man named Buckeye Summerville or any outstanding warrants for a woman named Rowena Jansen.'

'Who the devil are those two?' Sparky wanted to know.

'I would expect you to tell me, Spartan. You said he was down at the Keylock junction. Plus, you told me he was injured and could hardly ride.'

'That's the gospel truth! The man was about to fall off his horse.' Sparky tossed his head back and forth as if in agony and disbelief. 'I don't know how in blazes he got mixed up with someone named Buckeye and a female.'

Konrad chuckled. 'At least the woman has no warrants on her. You might count that as a blessing.'

'I've never seen a man who could get involved with other people so quick. I swear, the Capt'n was supposed to be in bed, getting rested up for the remainder of our trip. It's getting so I can't leave that boy for a minute!'

'Let's walk over to the judge's office and I'll get those warrants for you. To make all of this legal, I'll expect you to wear a badge and contact me when you've made the arrests.'

'Yeah, yeah, I know how this works, Marshal. I'm your patsy.'

'Just wanted to make sure you remembered the rules. Not much has changed since the last time you worked for me.'

'That was before the war. I'm surprised you're still walking around with a badge on your chest.'

'I'm getting married next month, a lady I met a couple years back. She's still got kids to raise, so I'll have to find time to try and be a father.'

Sparky smiled. 'Well, kiss my mare and call her

your mama! That's just fine, Marshal. I mean it. I wish you all the best.'

'Just don't call me into a situation where I get myself killed. All right?'

'You got my promise,' Sparky replied. 'Me and the Capt'n will handle whatever comes up. The only thing you will have to do is take credit for our good work.'

Konrad responded with a dry cynicism. 'That's something I'm truly looking forward to, Spartan.'

Sparky winked. 'Trust me, Marshal. I'll make you proud.'

Neville talked to the gal while Waco was nursing a beer at a table by himself. Neville had been buying drinks and socializing with Sally-Mae for nearly two hours. No one knew her last name, or if Sally-Mae was even her real first name, but she was one of the few women bar owners he'd come across. Oh, there were a good many small taverns, trading posts or the like, where a woman did the serving, but the saloon in Keylock had gambling tables, a roulette wheel and even a piano player. It was about as high class as anyone would find between Denver and Salt Lake.

'Yes, we all know about the renegade out in the hills,' Sally-Mae was saying. 'I treated a gent who had a run-in with the thief.' A coarse laugh. 'He looked like a full-sized steer had done a dance on his face. Busted his nose and blacked both eyes.' Another laugh.

'He said it was an Indian?'

Sally-Mae winked. 'He wouldn't admit that some half-wild squaw did that much damage to his face. Of course, I'm sure it was the female thief. Who else would steal a bonnet and leave berries or skinned rabbits for the food they took?'

'Anyone else ever seen her?'

'Not to my knowledge.'

'Where does this cowpoke live?' Neville asked. 'We'd sure like to talk to him.'

'Their ranch is about four miles west of town, just south of the creek. From what I've heard, they only have a shack and corral, but they earn enough to survive. Tibbs and Ponch are the only names I know them by.'

Neville put a couple dollars on the bar. 'Thanks a lot, Sally-Mae,' he said, showing his best smile. 'We'll ride out that way tomorrow and have a talk with them.'

Sally-Mae picked up the money and smiled back. 'Sure thing, honey. I'm always glad to help.'

'I'm turning in,' Neville told Waco, who had not budged from drinking alone at a corner table. 'Don't drink up all of our money.'

'No, sir, boss. I'll be along in a little while.'

Neville strode for the batwing doors, his teeth clenched with the effort required to hold back his ire. The girl was close. He would question the cowboys and find out where she was holed up. Then . . . then she would be damned sorry she had clouted him over the head and killed his brother!

Travis was watching the road and spied Sparky, still leading their extra mount, coming down the trail late in the afternoon. He rode his horse over to intercept his friend and explained the situation about the girl.

'Let me get this straight,' Sparky said, once he had finished. 'This new-found friend of yours is running from a man who helped to kill her guardian or adopted father – whatever this Buckeye character was to her – because she kilt his brother.'

'That's about the size of it.'

'And she's been living off the land and hiding out here in the hills for the past coupla months?'

'Uh-huh.'

'And now you figure we ought to take her with us and find her a place to live?'

'She don't have anyone else to help her, Sergeant.'

Sparky snorted. 'Yeah, you only call me *Sergeant* when we're fixing to get into a fight and you figure I can't say no to a commanding officer.'

130

'Neville Pockman won't be alone. They had a man working for them. And if he learns we're helping the young lady, he will likely get more help.'

'Man alive, Capt'n!' Sparky whined. 'Didn't you think we already had enough of a chore on our hands? I mean, you're so stove-up you can hardly ride and I'm an old man. It was a big enough chore for the two of us to take on the entire crew of the Diamond A ranch. Now you go and find us another battle to fight?'

'Strategy, my good friend,' Travis said, displaying a serene confidence. 'With a superior strategy in place, we can win both battles.'

Sparky had worked up a lather, fretting and apprehensive, but when Travis spoke with such a relaxed conviction, it was like a mother hushing a fussy baby. He swallowed his concerns and eyed his friend with wonderment.

'I'm listening, Capt'n,' he said, after a short pause. 'What's the plan?'

Travis explained what he had in mind while leading Sparky toward the girl's cave. They tied off the animals in the cove where they were out of sight from the road below or the trail going to Silver Crest. Then the two of them made the climb up the hill to the hiding-place.

Rowena had a stew in the pot and was wearing

her buckskin skirt and worn yellow blouse. Sparky took but one look and he knew why Travis was intent upon rescuing the young lady.

'Nice place you have here,' Sparky greeted her, looking around the interior of the cave. 'From the lack of furniture, I'd guess you don't entertain guests very often.'

'You're only the second guest to ever come here,' she said softly, too shy to make eye contact.

'Name's Spartan Vogel, but most everyone calls me Sparky,' he introduced himself.

'Sparky and I have been together since '61,' Travis told her. 'After the war, we went to work on his sister and brother-in-law's ranch. We need to get back the money that was lost or the place might go broke.'

'I remember you telling me about it,' Rowena said. 'Stew's hot, if you're hungry.'

'It smells like heaven to me,' Sparky said. 'I ain't et since last night.'

'Soon as we finish eating, we'll put the plan in motion,' Travis said.

'Aye, Capt'n,' Sparky replied, displaying a wide grin. 'It'll be just like we was back fighting those Johnny Rebs.'

Travis and Sparky covered some details of what needed to happen and he then watched his friend

132

start off toward Keylock.

This was a daring move, but it seemed the best chance to protect the girl and possibly get something back for the stolen cattle. As for the deaths of Hayes and Riley, that score would have to be settled as well.

Travis returned to the cave but stopped at the entranceway. He pulled the curtain back to see Rowena sitting with her knees up under her chin and her arms wrapped about her legs. She was rocking back and forth and humming – it sounded like a lullaby.

He stepped inside, but she didn't seem to notice him. She was staring blankly at the wall, as if in another world.

Travis remembered the girl's tale, about her capture and how she had pretended to be crazy. This appeared to be something like a defensive posture, a withdrawing inside herself for protection and isolation. Rather than speak to her and interrupt her concentration, he moved over next to her and sat down.

Several minutes passed before Rowena suddenly spoke.

'I sometimes get frightened,' she murmured softly. 'I try to be strong and brave, like the nice lady told me, but it doesn't always work.'

Travis slipped his good right arm about her

shoulders, pulling her a little closer. 'I have some idea of how you must have felt,' he said, his voice a mere whisper. 'Often, before a battle, I would retreat into my own private world. I would day-dream about riding my favorite horse across an open meadow, or lying in the sun and watching the clouds drift lazily overhead. I would try and remember times that were tranquil and safe, so I didn't have to think about the killing and dying that was imminent.'

'It was so cold,' Rowena whimpered, staving off a sob. 'And we had almost no water or food. Then the braves would come and take some of the women or girls away.' She visibly swallowed the terror of the memory. 'And I was alone, so very alone.'

Travis tightened his grip about her shoulders. 'You're not alone any more, Rowena,' he told her tenderly. 'We're in this together, and everything is going to turn out fine.'

The girl's head lifted and she gazed directly into his eyes. He met the perusal with a steady look of his own, knowing she was searching for any shred of doubt or fear. Seeing his stolid determination and also his unmasked desire, a slender smile rose to her lips.

'Buckeye told me I was old enough that I should have already been kissed by some young whelp who wished to court me proper.'

'He did, huh?'

'I never pictured anyone like you, 'cause you're probably experienced and all.'

'I admit, I've kissed a woman or two . . . though I was never serious about courting them proper.'

She lowered her eyelids, shielding him from her anxiety. 'I seen a couple of people kissing one time,' she admitted. 'Seemed to be a right pleasurable thing, too.'

'It can be, if you truly care for the one you're kissing.'

Rowena subtly moistened her lips and said, 'I've become right fond of you, Mr Clay.'

'And you're the sweetest girl I ever met, Miss Jansen.'

She didn't speak again, but closed her eyes and turned her head slightly toward him. Travis cupped her chin in his free hand and gently kissed her.

After a short pause, so she didn't think him an impetuous brute, he kissed her a second time, lingering a few moments longer. Then he sat back and waited for her reaction.

Rowena glanced up at him and smiled. 'Do this mean you wish to court me, Mr Clay?'

'Yes, ma'am!' he said emphatically. 'It means exactly that.'

'Then we can commence with first names. Buckeye told me how only an honorable man

135

should ever be allowed to call me by my first name. Walt done stepped all over being proper, cause he didn't have no honor or manners.'

'Well, I'd be honored to call you Rowena and have you call me Travis.'

She leaned in close and laid her head against his chest. 'I'm still scared,' she murmured softly. 'But being held is a whole lot better than rocking and singing.'

'I like your singing,' Travis told her. 'But I'll admit, holding you close – this is the best time I can ever remember.'

'For me too,' she replied. 'I feel a whole lot better now.'

CHAPTER ELEVEN

'I don't like it,' Waco spoke his mind. 'How did that teeny little bobcat manage to find so much help?'

Neville shook his head. 'It don't sound too bad. A ranch with only four or five hands. That ain't much of a ranch.'

'Four or five men is a heck of a lot more than you and me!'

'We can even the odds if we get those two morons we talked to yesterday to join us. You heard what they said: they want to get even with the girl and the character she joined up with. When I told them we intended to see both of them dead, they didn't back water one bit.'

'We should have gone looking for the gal instead

of wasting time talking to those two. We might have caught them before they left for the ranch.'

'That opportunity is gone, Waco. We can only get help and go after them now.'

'Yes, but Tibbs is half-blind with the swelling around his eyes and Ponch ain't playing with a full deck. You hear him laugh? He sounds like a wind-broke jackass!'

'It's two more guns,' Neville maintained. 'Rowena is bound to reach the ranch before we catch up. We're going to need them.'

'All right. It's your call. You want 'um, we'll bring 'um along. I'm just saying, those best be ordinary cowhands we're talking about. Because if they put up a fight, we're in over our heads.'

'It's going to be easy, Waco. We'll hit them when they ain't expecting no trouble. By the time they realize we mean business, we'll have either taken Rowena or have shot them to pieces.'

'You sure we want to do something this big?' Waco asked. 'What about the law? If we have to kill several men, there will be some kind of investigation.'

'You heard Tibbs last night. They don't have any law this side of Denver, except for the US marshal. And he has all of Colorado and Wyoming to cover. They don't look at simple range wars or the occasional murder here or there, because they don't have the manpower. That there ranch is so far away it'll be written off as an attack by a few renegade Indians or something. Soon as we deal with the gal, we'll head back for our neck of the woods. Ain't no one going to be looking for us.'

'You know I'm with you, right or wrong,' Waco said. 'I ain't got nowhere else to go. A few more killings won't trouble my conscience. I'm already headed to hell when this life is over.'

Neville shrugged. 'I never picked up a Bible and I ain't gonna ask for forgiveness for my sins. Guess you and I will take that last road together too.'

Waco chuckled. 'Yeah, and Walt will be there to welcome us both.'

Two days of hard riding put them at the ranch. Travis felt some stiffness, but he no longer had the jabbing pain every time he moved his left arm. The Nalens were happy to see them, although they were saddened by the deaths of Hayes and Riley. Plus, there was the loss of payment for a hundred head of beef. That put the ranch's survival in jeopardy.

'We've a plan to get it back,' Sparky informed Abe after everyone had settled in. Hannah had made up a bed for Rowena in the single room once occupied by their three girls. The two of them were out of the room, so Travis told Abe about the plan.

'You really think it will work?' Abe asked, once he had the details.

'There will be at least four of them,' Travis replied. 'We have to deal with them as best we can.'

'And afterwards?'

'We extract the money from Armstrong. Sparky has warrants for the four who ambushed us. If we have to, we'll take the payment out in beef. At last count, I believe he had over two hundred head of cattle.'

'How long before the men chasing after the lady get here?'

'We'll have to be on guard from now on. It could be any time.'

'I'll take the first watch,' Sparky volunteered. 'I reckon that Nanny Goat Ridge would be the best place, Capt'n. How about you spell me around midnight?'

'First sign of them, we need to act,' Travis replied. 'This is going to be like our war days, outnumbered and outgunned.'

'Aye, Capt'n,' Sparky said, displaying a grin. 'But so long as we ain't *outsmarted*, we'll get through this.'

'I'll see you about midnight. Be sure no one sees you or we could be in real trouble.'

Sparky snorted, 'Not to worry. I'll be as invisible

as a gnat after dark.'

After rounding up some food and filling his canteen Sparky rode off in the direction of Nanny Goat Ridge. Abe stood alongside Travis and watched for a time. When he spoke, the concern was heavy in his voice.

'I had hoped to escape any bloodshed,' he said. 'When you and Sparky arrived a few years back it was like getting a new start on life. Armstrong backed down from his pushing and we were living in peace.'

'The man didn't back down, he changed his strategy,' Travis replied. 'He lulled us to sleep and hit us without warning. We underestimated how ruthless and determined he was.'

The sorrow was evident in Abe's voice. 'Riley and Hayes had been with me since I started the place. They were good old boys who did their jobs without complaint and I never had to worry about the cattle.'

Travis added to their praise. 'They taught me everything I needed to know and never once resented you making me ramrod of the spread. I only survived the attack out of dumb luck, the fact the bullet somehow missed my heart. Even then, I'd have died if not for Sparky. He saved my life.'

Abe's expression grew dark. 'Armstrong has to pay for those murders, even if we never get a dime back for our lost herd.'

'Believe me, boss,' Travis vowed, 'they are all going to pay for their crime. And the same thing goes for the men chasing Rowena. Those kinds of people seem to think that because there's no sheriff here, they can get away with murder, kidnapping and rape. I aim to show them the error of such notions.'

In an odd show of solidarity, Abe reached out to shake Travis's hand. 'Whatever you have to do – whatever you need us to do – me and Hannah are behind you one hundred per cent.'

After supper, Travis went to lie down, hoping to get some sleep before going to relieve Sparky. He had just gotten comfortable in the bunkhouse when the sound of soft steps caused him to sit up.

Rowena wavered a moment, then hurried over and sat down by his side. He didn't say anything, waiting for her to speak.

'I've never felt this way before,' she said softly. 'Buckeye thought his heart was giving out, so I feared he might die and leave me on my own. But he was like an uncle to me. It didn't worry me so much that I couldn't sleep.'

'We have a plan, Rowena,' Travis told her gently. 'And part of the plan is that no one takes you away or hurts you.'

A tight little frown came to her face. 'I ain't

worried about me, silly. I've still got Walt's gun and I'll keep a handful of rocks handy. It's you I'm thinking of.'

Travis put an arm around her shoulders and she cuddled up next to him. 'My not getting killed is also part of the plan.'

'What's going to happen after this is over?' she asked. 'I mean, I don't know how I can pay these folks for taking care of me.'

'I kind of figured I would take care of you,' Travis said. Then added gently, 'And you could take care of me.'

'Not like Buckeye?' she said. 'I mean, I don't think of you as my uncle.'

Travis cupped her chin in his hand and turned her toward him so he could kiss her. After a moment, he smiled. 'I don't want you to think of me like Buckeye, Rowena. When this is over, I'd prefer to have you as my wife.'

The girl rotated around and slipped her arms around him. She sat that way for a long time, resting her head against his shoulder. After a few moments she pulled back enough to kiss him then she stood up.

'That's what I needed to know, Travis. I think I'll be able to sleep now.'

He watched her turn and hurry from the bunkhouse. Having kissed her and felt her warm body against his own, he groaned happily.

Yeah, but how am I supposed to get any shuteye?

CHAPTER TWELVE

Neville moved up next to Waco and stared down at the ranch house below. There was a bunkhouse to one side and a barn at the other. To the rear was a large corral with several horses in it.

'Sun will be up in a few minutes,' Waco said. 'I seen someone moving around in the house. They are probably starting to prepare breakfast.'

'How about the bunkhouse?'

'Only man moving is the one who was up on the hill. He left his position a few minutes after daylight. I think he was a night guard.'

'Why would they have a man on watch?' Neville wondered aloud.

'Rowena likely told them we were looking for her. I'll bet he was keeping an eye out for us.'

Neville snorted his contempt. 'You're probably right, but them clowns are only expecting two of us.

I reckon they were concerned we might try and sneak in and grab the girl during the night.'

'The house is pretty big. I'll bet Rowena was given a room inside.'

'Got to wonder how many men are down there,' Neville got down to serious business. 'They won't be concerned about a major attack, 'cause they don't know we have help.'

Waco took another long look around. 'Just the one guard posted, so I'd say they aren't too worried.'

'Damn that woman!' Neville cursed vehemently. 'She would have to find help. Tibbs and Ponch said they only saw her with one man. But now she's got an entire ranch to defend her.'

'We can forget about her,' Waco suggested. 'We walk away and not look back.'

'I promised Tibbs a chance to get even.'

'So what?' Waco said. 'We didn't start out after Rowena with the idea of having to kill three or four men to get to her.'

But Neville had his mind made up. 'There's four of us and we've got surprise on our side. If we pick our time, hit them when they are weakest, we can take over the ranch long enough to grab Squirrel and vamoose.'

'You think they might give her up without a fight?' Waco queried.

'Once the men leave to tend the cattle, we'll only have a couple left to deal with. They won't be any trouble, whether they decide to fight or not.'

'Any sign of that jasper I told you about, the one who attacked me?' Tibbs wanted to know, having crawled up next to them. 'He's got to be down there.'

'We don't know what he looks like,' Neville stated the obvious, 'but it's likely he's in the bunkhouse. From the number of horses and what we learned from that guy in Keylock, there's at least four or five men on the place.'

Tibbs pulled his pistol and checked the loads. 'Ponch and I are ready. Are we clear about the girl?'

'We'll stick to our end of the deal,' Neville assured him. 'We help kill the fellow who attacked you and anyone else who gets in the way. Then we grab the girl and head for the hills. You do whatever you want to her, but I'm the one who finishes the job.'

Tibbs uttered a vicious chortle. 'Yeah, Ponch and me will leave enough for you to have your revenge.'

'She murdered my brother, stabbed him right through the heart. I won't rest till she gets the same treatment.'

'They are getting up!' Waco sounded the alarm. 'A couple of them are coming out of the bunkhouse.'

Neville dug an elbow into Tibbs. 'You and Ponch get the horses ready. Soon as the riders head out for the day, we'll jump the others and find the squaw woman.'

Tibbs hesitated before leaving. 'Just watch for a man wearing a black hat with a silver band. That'll be the joker I want.'

'If he is one of those who heads out to tend cattle, you'll have to figure another way to get him. The girl is our single concern.'

Tibbs gave a nod of understanding. 'Fine. Just call out if you see him.'

For the next hour the four raiders waited with their horses ready and watched the ranch. After breakfast at the main house three of the cowboys mounted up and left the ranch. A few minutes later, three others appeared outside the house.

'That's got to be everyone but the cook and Squirrel,' Neville said. 'Those cowboys who rode out should be out of hearing distance.'

'I don't see the one with the fancy black hat,' Tibbs complained.

'We can't wait no longer,' Neville said. 'Let's hit 'um hard!'

The trio of men had undoubtedly been discussing the day's work or just passing time. Before they realized they were under attack, gunfire shattered the still morning air.

148

One man was struck twice and went down without a fight. A second was hit in the back, but managed to crawl to the side of the house. The third got off one shot, before he was hit in the thigh. He ran, staggering for the bunkhouse, dragging his injured leg. It looked as if the bold attack had worked.

However, the bunkhouse was not empty. Two guns suddenly opened fire from a window, both shooting rifles. At the same time, another gun belched fire from within the house.

Ponch had been out in front of the group. He took the brunt of the first volley of gunfire and was knocked from the saddle, riddled with several bullets.

Waco hit the ground running and charged the porch, thinking to break through the front door, but a bullet hit him high in the chest and stopped him cold at the front step. A second round folded him in the middle and he collapsed to the ground.

Neville jumped down from his horse and took up a position behind a water trough. He fired until his gun was empty and ducked down to reload. Then he saw Tibbs slump forward on his horse. The injured man neck-reined hard, attempting to retreat, but he couldn't stay in the saddle. He spilled like a sack of grain on to the dusty ground. Rising up to his hands and knees, Tibbs crawled for cover. . . .

He was too slow. The rifleman in the house pumped three bullets into him. Tibbs died in front of Neville's eyes.

Everything bad had happened quickly. The ambush should have caught the ranch hands totally off guard. There were only three mounts left in the corral. Where did all of the shooters come from?

Neville peeked over the trough and deduced what had happened. Behind the house were another three saddled horses, the same ones they had seen earlier. Those men had only pretended to ride off. They had circled and come back, slipping inside both the main house and the bunkhouse, sitting with guns at hand, lying in wait for any attack. The only reason any of the people from the ranch were hit was because they hadn't expected Neville and the others to ride in shooting. Angry at the brutality of the assault, the surviving men were out for blood.

Ponch, Tibbs and Waco were all dead. Neville looked for a route of escape, but several shooters kept him pinned down. He had a loaded gun, but could not get off a shot. After a few terrifying moments the gunfire stopped. He risked a quick glance around the side of the trough and fear tore at his heart. Three men were moving toward him, all with their guns poised and ready to fire. He could try and take one or two of them, but three armed men at one time was suicide!

'You're done, mister,' one of the men snarled the words. 'We never figured you for such a foolhardy charge. We were going to have two more men pretend to ride out so you would think there was only me still on the place. Well, you killed at least one of my men and wounded a couple more, but we got you now.'

Neville wished Walt was here. He always had a head for a fight. He knew how to plan something. Neville had always followed his lead. Maybe that was the only move he had left, to follow his brother once more.

One of the armed men taunted him. 'Make your play or we'll shoot you where you're sitting, hunkered down like a frightened little kid.'

Neville rose up quickly, hoping to surprise them with the suddenness of his response—

Three guns blasted away at him. It was like standing up in a hail storm, but instead of balls of ice, it was numerous lead missiles that tore through Neville's body. He didn't have a chance to squeeze off a round from his pistol. His knees buckled and he flopped straight down. His upper body landed in the watering trough, his head going under the surface. Neville gagged from his single breath, due to inhaling a mouthful of foul liquid. It was the last sensation he felt.

Travis heard the approach of a horse. He glanced over his shoulder and saw Sparky had arrived. His eyes were still red from the short night.

'Heard the shooting a long way off,' was Sparky's greeting. 'Sounded like a regular war.'

'It was a fast and furious exchange, Sergeant. Rowena can rest easy from now on. Tibbs and Pockman, plus their two pals, are all down.'

'What about Armstrong's bunch?'

'Looked like one was killed and at least two more were wounded.'

'That gives us a little better odds.'

'They will send one man for the doctor,' Travis said. 'We'll take him first.'

'Old Mack Percy will be the one they call on. He lives this side of White River. We can grab the rider on the river trail.'

Travis pointed. 'Yep, there goes one of them toward those saddled mounts in back of the house. Looks like Jubal. The two wounded men are in the bunkhouse. One was hit in the upper leg. The other caught a slug in his back or shoulder, couldn't tell which, but they had to carry him to the bunkhouse.'

'Who else is on their feet?'

'Armstrong and Deetz. I think that only leaves the cook.'

'Aye, Capt'n, and their cook is an old Mexican woman. I've seen her once or twice. She lives over on the other side of the river.'

'Let's get a move on. We don't want Jubal to get past us.'

They mounted up, and after taking it easy down the hill for the sake of Travis's wound, made good time to the river trail. In less than ten minutes, Jubal Rhine came galloping for the doctor. He was going fast enough not to notice the rope tied across his path between two trees until it hit him in the chest.

Jubal was suspended for a split second as the horse ran out from under him, then he was flipped upside down, landing on his head and shoulders. Sparky ran from cover to put him under his gun while Travis caught up the man's horse.

Travis returned to see Sparky standing over the man with a sheepish look on his face. 'What?' he asked.

'It seemed a good idea, Capt'n,' Sparky said. 'Can't fault me because it didn't work as planned.'

'What are you talking about?'

Sparky sighed dejectedly and stepped out of the way. It allowed Travis to see that Jubal's head was cocked at an odd angle. That and the fact that his eyes were wide open and staring blindly.

'He's dead?'

'Broke his neck like snapping a twig,' Sparky

admitted. 'Must have unhorsed a dozen men like this before and never had one die from it.'

'Well, nothing we can do about it now, but it's going to look bad on your report to the marshal.'

'I was hoping Jubal would point a finger at Armstrong for being a part of the ambush and cattle rustling. If we don't get one of the others to say he ordered it, the man might get a pass on this whole thing.'

'Any way he wouldn't be involved?' Travis asked Sparky.

'Not a chance.'

'Let's load Jubal on his horse. We'll leave him with our mounts while we slip in and try to arrest the others.'

'OK, but I'm just saying, it ain't my fault that Jubal broke his neck.'

'We should have been ready!' Armstrong swore. 'The telegram from your cattle buyer said a couple men from the Nalen place were tracking you.'

'I didn't figure on Nalen getting so much help,' Deetz lamented. 'We rode directly to the railhead and sold the cattle. Then we brought the money back here like you said. We didn't spend but one night at a saloon, and I only give the boys a hundred each. Again, that's what you told me to do.'

'So where did Nalen get these four men? I've

never seen any of them before.'

'I don't know, boss, but he sure didn't hire them for brains. They could have slipped in during the night and taken us all. Instead, they come riding in like some kind of cavalry charge, right out in the open.'

'Nalen must have told them we were a bunch of greenhorns. They obviously came here expecting a turkey shoot.'

'They still did a lot of damage. Can't stop the bleeding of Tub's leg and Zig don't look like he'll make it.'

'Zig was always a good hand,' Armstrong pointed out. 'I hate to think he won't pull through.'

'Zig has always been tough, but a bullet in the back is never a good thing. I don't know if that old army medic is going to do him any good.'

'We'll just have to. . . .' But Armstrong caught the movement out of the corner of his eye. 'Cover!' he shouted, jerking his gun from its holster.

'Hold it!' Travis called the warning. 'You're under arrest!'

Deetz reacted like a snake with a stepped-on tail. He spun about and drew his gun too.

Sparky had them both under his rifle, as did Travis. But there was no choice. They both opened fire as the two men tried to shoot back. Fortunately for them, Sparky's aim was at Armstrong, while

Travis was more worried about Deetz, who was supposed to be very good with a gun.

Sparky's first shot spun Armstrong around, while Travis's hit Deetz dead center. Armstrong got off one shot, but it went wild. Sparky's second round dropped the man. Deetz tried to recover from being hit, lifting his pistol to return fire.

Travis had no choice but to drill him again. This time he sank to the ground and flopped on his back. In less than a half-dozen shots the fight was over. Both Deetz and Armstrong lay dead.

Sparky carefully entered the door to the bunkhouse, but he didn't have to fear being shot. Tub Boyle and Zig were both unconscious from their wounds. Sparky set about tending to them but it was too late to help either one.

Travis entered the house and found where Armstrong had hidden his money. There was close to $2,000 in a locked box. It was a lot less than the rustled cattle had been worth, but his men had unloaded them on the first buyer who offered them cash money. Of course, they could settle for the difference by taking some of Armstrong's cattle. Whatever was left would go to the mortgager of the Diamond A ranch.

The Mexican cook seemed unperturbed by the whole affair. She sat quietly at the table while Travis broke open the box and counted the money. When he had finished he asked the woman, 'How much do you earn a month?'

'Ten dollars,' she answered.

Travis gave the Mexican woman a hundred. 'Here's enough to tide you over until you find something else.'

She gratefully accepted the cash and left without a word.

Travis rejoined Sparky in the yard and informed him about the money and paying the cook. Sparky reported that there would be no survivors to haul off to jail.

'I don't know how I'm going to tell Marshal Ellington about this,' he whined. 'We've got bodies all over the place and neither of the wounded men will last out the day.'

'All of them were due a hangman's noose,' Travis pointed out. 'And most of them killed each other.'

'Oh, yeah,' Sparky said. 'I'm sure that will make it all better. I just have to explain how I gave some misinformation to four kidnappers so they would try to kidnap a girl from the *wrong* ranch. Next, I wired the six murdering rustlers to expect trouble from some gunmen *hired* by Nalen. Then I'd add how the one man I did capture *accidentally* broke his neck, and that you and I shot the only two still standing – without even getting a confession from Armstrong!'

157

Travis laughed. 'Look on the bright side, Sparky, Konrad Ellington isn't likely ever to ask you to pin on a star for him again.'

His friend snorted his agreement. 'Let's get these bodies taken care of,' he suggested. 'I'll worry about Marshal Ellington; you can worry about the little gal waiting for you back at the ranch.'

'I don't aim to worry her again. Soon as we get a house built, I'm going to marry her.'

'Be good for you, Capt'n,' Sparky said back to Travis. 'I'm getting too old to keep watching over you all the time. Be a comfort knowing someone else is there to do the job.'

'I couldn't have put it better myself, Sparky. No siree. That sounds just fine.'